UP FOR AIR

This Half Has Never Been Told!

IMANI M. TAFARI-AMA

Second Edition

Beaten Track

www.beatentrackpublishing.com

Second Edition
First published 2014

This edition published by:
Beaten Track Publishing
beatentrackpublishing.com

CATALOGING IN PUBLICATION DATA

Tafari-Ama, Imani M.

Up for Air: This Half Has Never Been Told!
By Imani M. Tafari-Ama
Second Edition

Includes Introduction and Ten Chapters.
1, Dancehall. 2, Politics. 3, Violence. 4, Jamaica. 5, Tivoli Gardens.
6, Religion. 7, Power. 8, Crime. 9, Corruption. 10, Inner-City.
11, Security Forces. 12, Gender. 13, Domination. 14, Agency.
I, Title.

Print ISBN: 978-1-78645-514-7
eBook ISBN: 978-1-78645-515-4

Beaten Track Publishing,
Burscough, Lancashire, United Kingdom.
www.beatentrackpublishing.com

Contents

Introduction

THE STORMING OF Tivoli Gardens by the security forces in May 2010 was an assault on the sensibilities of all Jamaicans, no matter which sector of our highly stratified society. We experienced the extraordinary standoff between the Jamaican and United States of America's governments over the extradition request by the latter for then Tivoli Don, Christopher "Dudus" Coke. We also watched with great anticipation, the televised Manatt, Phelps, and Phillip Inquiry, which cost some $78 million of public money to pay high-profile lawyers without a decisive result. It not being a legal trial, no one was held criminally responsible, so victims and sympathizers were unable to assuage their outrage. Everyone in Jamaica was acutely aware of the crescendo of events that culminated in this action and resulted in numerous deaths, damage to property, and widespread violation of human rights and material property.

Former Member of Parliament of the Tivoli Gardens community and its West Kingston environs, Edward Seaga was disparaging of then Prime Minister Bruce Golding's handling of the incident and suggested openly that more—perhaps double—the estimated seventy-three civilians were killed by the security forces.

I started doing content analysis of news items on the Tivoli Gardens Incursion and noted that, three years after the incident, when public advocate Lloyd D'Aguilar led a protest march to Jamaica House to deliver a petition with 2,000 signatures demanding an inquiry into the Incursion, Tamara Scott-Williams wrote a significant article (*Jamaica Observer*, March 24, 2013), calling out both People's National Party and Jamaica Labour Party representatives as carrying blood on their hands as far as citizen security in the Tivoli Gardens community was concerned. She cited the 1997 and 2001 bloodlettings in Tivoli as the dangerous precedents that set the stage for the 2010 human hemorrhage. She referred to Claude McKay's "If we Must Die" poem as her point of departure for critiquing the relevant institutions, particularly the Public Defender's office, for tardiness and insensitivity to the suffering of those who experience the power wielded by the Executive Arm of the State.

I also noted that just before the march on Jamaica House, there was an escalation in violence in the Tivoli Gardens community. According to senior writer at *The Gleaner*, Gary Spalding, "Over a four-week period, more than twelve persons, including two pregnant teens, were killed in the area around Tivoli Gardens, Denham Town and Matthews Lane" (*The Gleaner*, March 10, 2013). This upsurge resulted from relatives of former "strong men" jostling to reinstate the power of their fearsome family names. This struck me forcefully, since five pregnant women had been murdered in Jamaica in 2012, making the murder of the two pregnant teens mentioned in this report seem like common assault.

I remember a time, not so long ago, when pregnant women embodied the sacred, as symbolic and real life-givers, but ever since the "September 1 [2012]" incident in which "St Thomas police Corporal Dwayne Smart allegedly shot and killed pregnant Kay-Ann Lamont in Yallahs Square" (*The Gleaner*, November 1, 2012), this sacred symbol has been reduced to virtual ashes. This is emblematic of the loss of respect for human life generally, and females in particular, by the faceless gunmen wielding legal and illegal (masculinist) power over the society.

An article written by Anastasia Cunningham (*The Gleaner*, May 22, 2011), also noted that "studies revealed that 10 to 30 percent of the children in Tivoli Gardens, as many as 600, were greatly affected [by the Incursion] and might have developed or are developing post-traumatic stress disorder (PTSD) that will require ongoing intervention." This article emphasized the scant attention given by the relevant authorities to the plight of the vulnerable residents of Tivoli Gardens, who suffer the psychosocial and material fallout of the four-day siege.

I was moved to write this novella about the Tivoli Gardens Incursion because I felt the need to add to the growing protest movement against state-endorsed police brutality in Jamaica (Mutabaruka, Jerry Small, Isis, et al.), alongside the Rastafari Council, which organized the commemorative march in the politically busy month of March 2013, to honor those who have been brutalized by the Jamaican State. Somehow, every instance of police brutality against citizens in Jamaica is connected to the historically class-specific responses of the state to the majority of the population.

The *Up for Air* portion of the title symbolizes my positionality as a writer, releasing the bonds imposed on my creative imagination by many years of slavish project writing. It brings to the surface a self for too long submerged by orthodox models of self-representation finding release in a medium of expression that allows total freedom to imaginatively extrapolate from the facts. This approach is really a call for acknowledgement of the shocking realities that are staring us in the face but to which we responded with studious silence simply because we may not have constructed the appropriate vernacular for such forbidden subjects.

The first part of the title also addresses the human condition of powerlessness and of citizen insecurity; that people like the residents of Tivoli Gardens are virtually drowning because of the combination of disadvantages that they face—poverty, violence, and

SILENCE about their circumstances. The characters I constructed to provide virtual testimonies of their experiences around the Incursion should therefore be seen as only partial victims because they also embody the symbolic phoenix, rising from the ashes, crying their pain in the wilderness of paucity of political will, surviving by any means necessary.

The second half of the title—*This Half Has Never Been Told*—alludes to the fact that although the Tivoli Gardens Incursion was a watershed that forever changed the course of events in Jamaica and not only Tivoli Gardens, the truths about this event are still shrouded in the delayed official response. At the time of writing, in the summer of 2011, the Public Defender's report was outstanding; when I did the first revision of the draft in the spring of 2013, the interim report had been submitted to Parliament after myriad delays caused by lack of human resources. By press time, spring 2014, the three-person commissioner body had been identified to preside over a public inquiry into the event in response to one of the Public Defender's recommendations.

Like other concerned Jamaicans, I felt frustrated by the way the whole episode was treated as a proverbial nine-day wonder. I was therefore moved to revisit the scene of the crime, so to speak, so that in the re-living and retelling, we can problematize the many ways we trash events of our life without critical analysis so as not to treat the derived lessons learned as guideposts.

Moreover, since the call for compensation is an ongoing one, I acknowledge that I am only running one leg in this relay of remembrance.

I therefore join with the makers of the rising cacophony of dissent in Jamaica, Land we Love, against human rights abuses and, through this medium, reinforce the call for deconstruction of the problems compounded by state complicity in the oppressions of the citizens of Tivoli Gardens. This novella joins the call for equal rights and justice for the cited citizens of Tivoli Gardens and for the realization of relevant forms of equal rights and justice.

Imani M. Tafari-Ama
May 10, 2014

Chapter One

LITTLE DID THE Passa Passa revelers realize that Wednesday night was going to be the last time the dancehall extravaganza would be staged on the West Kingston streets framing the Tivoli Gardens community. Up until May 2010, the Passa Passa dancehall exposition used to be a mixed social gathering, which started Wednesday night and went on until daylight on Thursday when the sun got too hot to sustain this exposé. Like its Rae Town Old Hits counterpart, showcased on Sunday nights, Passa Passa was mainly frequented by residents of inner-city communities but also attracted a wide range of uptown patrons as well as international visitors to Jamaica.

Passa Passa was the brainchild of the now infamous Christopher "Dudus" Coke, "The President," who was convicted of international racketeering and imprisoned for twenty-three years in the United States of America (USA) after being extradited from Jamaica. This street dance also garnered prestigious sponsorship and enabled a wide range of itinerant vendors to make a living. However, the two leading local newspapers, *The Gleaner* and *The Observer*, found themselves in hot water when they put that assumption in print. In its retraction, *The Observer* noted that the event was owned by Prodigal Entertainment Limited, which was incorporated under the Jamaican laws on October 8, 2006, under the directorship of Dylan Powe and O'Neil Miles.

The tabloid noted further that "the Miles family and Prodigal Entertainment have staged the Passa Passa event at 47 Spanish Town Road since Ash Wednesday 2003."

The extradition request for Coke sparked an extended standoff between the Jamaican and the USA in late 2009; the entire Jamaican society waited nervously, marking time, wondering what the outcome would be while the then Jamaica Labour Party (JLP) government led by Bruce Golding, who later resigned over the affair, stalled, and politically stumbled. Still, Passa Passa patrons took this standoff in their stride as they continued to party, believing that event would be outside of the pale of politics.

The video lights were as hot and bright as ever and so were the women and men jostling for coverage by cameramen who, like vultures, hovered for the graphic consumption of flesh. Seemingly hypnotized by the roving eye of technology, the dancers outcompeted each other to produce the latest dance moves. The cameraman massaged the flaunted egos, faithfully following flips, flops, whines, and choreographed wiggles in singular and plural forms from one section of the crowd to another.

Shielding himself with the camera as if for protection from exposure to the flesh of straight males and females and cross-dressed metrosexuals, he secured shot after moving shot, already visualizing the wild impact these images would make when reproduced on cable television stations.

The dancers were unaware, as was Coke—that his telephone conversations were being tapped by Drug Enforcement Agents (DEA) in the USA and would be used as evidence of involvement in drug and gun running, hence the extradition request. The Jamaican Government's hands were tied for an extended period. Eventually, they hired a prominent law firm, Manatt, Phelps, and Phillips to lobby the US Government to drop the extradition request and ease the potential political tension in Jamaica. Meanwhile, it was widely rumored that Coke was not only in charge of a vast local criminal network but was also the authority figure for the notorious Shower posse, said to be responsible for a host of illegal deeds in Jamaica and the USA.

Paradoxically, Coke was loved and feared because of his influence in the Tivoli Gardens community, where he used Robin Hood tactics to secure loyalty. Tivoli Gardens was a stronghold of the JLP, which formed the government of the day. It was therefore widely rumored that the Member of Parliament (MP) for the area, Prime Minister Bruce Golding, was hesitant to hand Coke over to the USA. This was understandable because of Coke's control over contracts and the securing of scarce votes in the community.

The Jamaican Government's discourse of resistance of the extradition request was that the tapping of Coke's phone constituted a violation of his constitutional rights.

Not to be deterred, the US Government applied political and diplomatic pressure; the cancellation of the visas of prominent social actors including politicians and musicians was only the tip of the iceberg. Wikileaks revelations were later to expose the depth of frost that had developed in relations between the two countries over the affair. For example, significant political and popular artistic figures suddenly lost their American visas and then Prime Minister Golding threw thinly veiled barbs at the Washington capital during the Commission of Inquiry into the Manatt, Phelps, and Phillips' controversy.

Of course, the Passa Passa crowd was oblivious to the noose hanging over the head of the carousing feature of the Tivoli Gardens community. On that fateful night, at exactly midnight, the resident deejay announced that a competition would be held to select the "wickedest and wildest" male and female dancers. He described how contestants would be judged based on choreographic skill, outfits, and the closest simulation of dry sex moves. He did not need to elaborate what he meant for regular patrons, but he acknowledged visitors might wonder what he meant by "dry sex" and explained that in the dancehall, dancers pretended to be having sex as part of their performance, a creative skill that provided enjoyment for revelers and voyeurs alike.

Excitement buzzed with his announcement; the air virtually crackled with the waves of sound that rippled up in response to his call. The crowd went wild when the deejay declared that first-place winner would receive fifteen thousand dollars, second place ten thousand, and third place five thousand, courtesy of The President. The revelers usually danced for free every week, so the prospect of pay almost caused a stampede. Poverty was the familiar bedfellow of the majority of patrons present.

The deejay screamed for a full minute straight to hear himself over the din. Finally, he edged his voice over the chorus plying the thick atmosphere and demanded that all those who wanted to compete should line up in front of the huge stage imported onto the street for the occasion. It blocked the traffic that usually snaked its way through the crowd. Complying with this request required tremendous discipline since the revelers weren't used to forming a line for anything. It also took great stamina for those in the front to keep their pride of place.

For the next hour, music overtook the deejay's voice, and several popular dancehall favorites from artists including Vybz Kartel, Mavado, Beenie Man, Lady G, Elephant Man, Bounty Killa, Capelton, Sizzla, Lady Saw, and Tanya Stephens boomed over the sound boxes placed at strategic points on the main and adjoining streets. Finally, at exactly one o'clock, after much anticipation, the deejay announced the contest was about to begin.

The first dancer was a woman dressed in a red bikini outfit and black stiletto ankle boots. The front of the panties was daringly French cut, while a slim G-string was the flimsy attachment to the backside. She gyrated skillfully on hands, all fours, and her stiletto-clad feet in a smooth break-dance rendition that drew appreciative howls from the crowd. She was followed in quick succession by three young men all dressed alike in pink hipster pants and white skin-fitting T-shirts. They also had on pink and white gentleman's shoes, which enabled them to whirl and tap dance with great flourishes. The crowd was a bit cooler in their reception to these three despite their immaculate choreography; the cross-dressing was not a display that could be publicly supported in this environment. Inner-city communities like Tivoli Gardens were viciously opposed to any suggestion of homosexuality and its various offshoots. And although many of the revelers were from uptown and did not mind and many inner-city residents were secretly noncommittal or even sympathetic, they all kept quiet because they did not want to be identified as empathizers, which could be fatal. With some relief, the crowd watched the trio depart and expectantly cheered on the next contestant.

For two hours more, the contest continued; the various displays were not for the fainthearted. Apart from the skimpy outfits which left little of the sex of the wearers to the crowd's imagination, the auto-arousal techniques as well as the partner performances of almost-but-not-quite sex literally took their breath away. As part of their creative output, some women stood on head tops and bared vaginas to the critical eyes of all and sundry. The climax of one such display came when a trio of two women and a man came on stage at around three-thirty. They started out with the man in the middle and the two women grinding on him, front and back, to the rhythmic insistence of Busy Signal's "Pon di Edge." Then, still moving to the rhythm, the front dancer unzipped the man's fly, dipped her hand inside, pulled out his rock-hard member and proceeded to give him a blow job.

The crowd went wild, egging her on, and the man responded by slamming her mouth with skillful gyrations of his own. The young woman in front, who appeared to be around eighteen years of age, was soon joined by her counterpart, who seemed equally juvenile. Shouts of "come inna dem mout" rippled across the crowd, and when the man complied, there was thunderous applause. No one seemed to notice that the trio had exceeded the one minute timeline; it was as if time had frozen.

Suddenly, one man shouted, "Dem two whore deh fi go a dem yaad!"

There was a deafening moment of silence, and then one of the girls said, "Move an go whey! How di rass you no call di man whore an a three a we you see up ya?" She assumed the body language of someone ready to trace (quarrel) or fight, and the other girl bellowed an unmistakable expletive adding sharply, "You a mussi battyman or jealous. Come up ya if yuh wood nuh dead an mek mi see wha you mek outa!"

"Go way, gyal. You can't put yuh frowzy mout pon my cocky!" the man retorted.

By this time, revelers began a murmur of discontent that was quickly rising to sound like anger. Someone close to the stage shouted, "A wha happen to the deejay?"

As if on cue, the deejay's voice boomed over the microphone, "We want to keep the vibes warm an easy inna the Passa Passa." He spoke soothingly, in contrast to his earlier stridency. "Nice an easy. Mek we see the other contestant come pon di stage right now."

Simultaneously, Tanya Stephens' "It's a Pity" crowded the airwaves. The intervention had the desired effect; the revelers simmered to an even keel once more, and the deejay exhorted, "Keep the sex dry, people. Things get too complicated when we wet up the situation."

Bawdy cheers greeted his comment as two young women mounted the stage. One was dressed in a sheer, black teddy type garment and matching knickers with knee-high black boots, while the other had on a body-hugging, ankle-length, halter-back, red dress with a slit on the left side up to the hip offering glimpses of red panties as she moved. The music flipped to Kartel's "Tek Buddy Gyal," and again the performance offered by the dancers edged over the norm to the risqué.

Without preamble, the red-dress-clad dancer did a headstand, and her gown fell around her head. With her legs spread, her vagina was revealed in the middle of crotchless panties. The other dancer sidled up to her and flung her left leg between her partner's while balancing on her right. It was amazing that both maintained rhythmic equilibrium, simulating sexual motion and not missing a step.

The videographers were having a field night of it. With apparent embarrassment, some tourist-looking patrons started to edge their way away from the floodlit stage area, clearly not wishing to be included in the explicit footage details.

Ringside viewers shouted various comments from "Sadamite" to "Onoo nuh hear Kartel say tek buddy, a wha dat?" Once more, pandemonium broke out in the crowd, and again the deejay had to rescue the situation.

"People," he implored, "we know dat all kind a ting gwaan inna di dancehall, but we want fi keep the vibes pon a level tonight. We want fi big up all the visitors and VIPs inna the place. Di President inna di residence too, so we want fi say maximum respect for the support and sponsorship of the dance contest. So mek we just a have some fun and keep it real, people."

While he spoke, the dancers disentangled and resumed singular stances and finally trotted off. Several individual female and male dancers alternated after that for the edge in the competition, and it was four-thirty when a husky male dressed in full black carrying a foam mattress under one arm mounted the stage.

This development attracted the commentary of the deejay once again, who announced, "It look like da bredda ya a go sort out some daggering fi wi tonite. A who him a go tek on now?"

As if controlled by remote, a young girl, no more than sixteen from the looks of her face and body, bounded onto the stage and threw herself down on the mattress. She was dressed in denim French-cut shorts, popularly called a batty rider, and a navy-blue tube top. The male dancer flung himself on top of her, evidently intent on grinding her into dust. She seemed up to the task, however; her spindly legs wrapped around the man's waist, and she heaved her pelvis in a mighty thrust and met stroke with stroke. The crowd went wild as the man spun the woman around and slammed his pelvis into her bumping and grinding buttocks as insistent strains of Mr. Vegas' "Daggering" rolled around the concrete lawn. At last, as the deejay faded down the tune, the man simulated the short stabbing movements of pre-orgasm and then, with a vicious thrust, collapsed on his companion, whose corresponding body language suggested they had scored simultaneously.

The deejay announced as they left the stage, "Well, crowd a people, that couple was the thirtieth act, and the police have just informed us that we have to break up the party for security reasons. So we have no choice but to announce the winners and clear the area. Apparently, an operation is going to be launched, and we are in the way of the officers. No disrespect officers of the law. We are just about to close the show."

Sounds of disappointment mushroomed from the crowd, and someone close to the stage yelled, "Dem eedyat police always know how fi spoil di fun, eeh?" Other mutterings concurred.

To maintain an even keel seemed to be the role the deejay was called upon to play, yet again. Sensing this, he slapped "Living Dangerously" by Barrington Levi and Bounty Killa on the turntable, and after it had played for two minutes, he faded the tune under his voice and announced that third-place winners were the daggering pair while the second-place winner was a young woman who, dressed in a white meshed dress, had done a routine that was a dancehall adaptation of Michael Jackson's "Thriller." Finally, he announced, "And the winner is..." A hush of anticipation fell on the crowd... "The fucking trio!"

From the combination of moans and screams, it was clear the crowd had mixed reactions of outrage and elation to this choice. From some of the comments that could be deciphered over the din, it seemed the source of discontent related to the moral view expressed earlier, which adversely judged the women involved while no such criticism was forthcoming for the man. On the other hand, a cry of "A real dancehall head dat dem give him!" which went up from one patron, summarized the supportive views of those who thought the trio was deserving of the coveted prize. However, voices of protest lingered. "Di deejay did say dry sex, but a wet sex dem gi wi. You neva see how di man wet up dem face?" The hot comments continued for some time as revelers screamed their angst.

As soon as the dancers had collected their prizes, the deejay voiced over Beenie Man's "Back it Up," announcing, "No disrespect to one, no disrespect to all, crowd a people. But as I said before, the dance done because the security forces want the area cleared immediately because they intend to carry out an operation.

Cutting into the deejay's announcement, the starched voice of a police official reiterated that the area had to be cleared within the hour and a curfew was to be imposed at six a.m. With that detail, it was as if he had waved a magic wand; the police were notorious for their violations of human rights, especially under curfew conditions. Within fifteen minutes of the announcement, the only signs of life in the previously thickly crowded area were the crew of workers deftly loading the sound boxes, technical equipment, and stage parts into two trucks, vendors heaving goods and equipment onto handcarts and into cars, and the dogs picking their way through scraps of food carelessly flung on the streets by the revelers. It was ten minutes to six when the truckers gunned their engines and lumbered off. The security operations in the West Kingston division to capture the elusive Coke had commenced.

Chapter Two

SOPHIA SIGHED AS she struggled up the fourth flight of stairs with the two bags of ground provisions she had just bought in the market, downtown Kingston. She vowed silently that this would be the final time she was going to be pregnant as a single parent. "At the end of the day," she muttered to herself as she let herself into her apartment on Building D in the Tivoli Gardens high-rise housing complex, "no matter how loving a man claimed to be, is just like the song say—promises at night are so easily made, but they can disappear at the light of day."

Sophia took going to the Passa Passa event on Wednesday nights as her break from the mundane, her chance to shine as a star under the video lights. Even now, when she was heavily pregnant, she felt the need to make her presence felt so people would not forget her. In the dancehall, new stars were born every day, dependent on who had the capacity for doing the most outrageous embodied feats, and she was famous for developing the side wine, where the dancer executed the most skillful hip gyrations while lying on his or (usually) her side in the dust or, if the dancer was more famous and serious, on a piece of cardboard.

While she had felt the usual electrical excitement in the first part of the dance, Sophia realized when she observed the younger dancers doing expert headstands and backflips that her stardom had waned. She could not imagine herself skinning out like some women did.

"A wha do dem, or a wha do mi?" she implored her friend Ruthie.

"Baby love, if you no raw, yuh no ready," was Ruthie's sanguine response.

As she made herself a cup of peppermint tea, Sophia acknowledged the death of her career as a dancehall hottie-hottie; she was also apprehensive about how the dance had ended. She had felt real fear grip her womb when the deejay announced the closing down of the sound and requested the dispersal of the crowd. Sophia suddenly heard her mother's voice in her memory warning, *"If a gate don't stop you, a wall will."* It seemed, she mused to herself, that the time had not only run out for the boss but for the community as a whole because she could not imagine what Wednesday nights were going to be like without Passa Passa. Who was she going to show off on? What was going to happen to all the people who depended on the dance and the boss to make a living?

As the baby kicked in her stomach, Sophia could not stop her thoughts from racing down bitterness avenue, where her feelings for her man dwelled. Nor could she stop the bile from rising in her throat as she reflected on the last night she had spent with Steve, her partner of the past two years. He had impregnated her eight and a half months before and then shocked her out of her wits in her sixth week by demanding a paternity test. The relationship had been strained ever since the results came back. Sophia felt she did not have what it would take to forgive him, and she sensed Steve was too ashamed to completely relax with her anymore. He tried to explain to her on several occasions that he had lost it because he was so anxious. This was his first successful pregnancy; on the previous two occasions, his former lovers had aborted before he got used to the idea of being a father, so he had trust issues that he still had not resolved.

In her head, Sophia understood, but in her heart, she was bitter. She did not enjoy being fried in other people's fat, and although she had three children previously by three different fathers, she was really a serial monogamist, as she said ruefully to friends and family members who wondered aloud why she kept getting pregnant.

"You can't fuck without breed?" her sister Diana asked in real anger. Her spirit did not take Steve anyway, but she'd also wanted to give him an uppercut over his paternity test request and only stopped short because of Sophia's own pleading.

Sophia was left with a feeling of apprehension as she contemplated the immediate future. Already she got signs of the shift in the matrix with Steve failing to help her with things like the shopping, which he used to do when love was new. Putting on the kettle to make another cup of tea, Sophia wiped away involuntary tears with the back of her hand as a wave of self-pity washed over her.

She was just about to drown in her sorrows when her cell phone rang. In something of a daze, she reached into her handbag and felt a surge of relief upon seeing her mother's number.

"Mama, wha you a say—" she started but was quickly interrupted by Sadie Baynes, who had not only mothered Sophia and her six siblings but also a host of others in the Tivoli Gardens community and beyond. Although Sadie had moved out a year earlier when her firstborn, Raymond, bought her a house in Old Harbour, she was often in the community visiting family and friends.

"A wha dat mi hear bout how Steve a treat you Sophia? How come you hide dem tings from me and me and you so close? Mi just deh ya a talk to you Aunitie Anita, and she a give me the whole bill and receipt. That bwoy is damn out of all order, and I have a good mind to tell him so myself. I always did tell you mi never think him was quite righted inna him head. Him tek after him mad mumma."

When Sadie paused momentarily to catch her breath, Sophia took her chance to get a word in, edgewise. "I am so glad you talked to Auntie Anita. I was just thinking I should ask if you can come and stay with me till the baby born because I just come back from Coronation Market, and it is really hard…" Her mother would know Sophia was going to start crying because her voice cracked as she said *hard*. Still, Sadie listened for another twenty seconds before interrupting.

"Save your credit, my daughter. You will see me around three o'clock. It is two o'clock now."

Ending the call, Sophia felt a wave of relief wash over her and sat on the red leatherette settee, noticing as she put her feet up that they were swollen. Going to the Passa Passa dance the night before and then heading straight to the market this morning had taken their toll. She could hear her mother's voice in her head saying, "Belly ooman can't do as she like. She haffi consider baby first." With the dance closed down under such tense circumstances, Sophia realized she needed to have a good talk with her mother, whom she could depend on to provide all the news behind the news.

Sadie Baynes, known to most people as Miss Sadie, had sold a variety of fruits and vegetables in Coronation Market for thirty-two years. Her occupation linked her to a wide network of communicants while providing her with an independent source of income to raise her children, singlehandedly. She was legendary for her fierce defense of her offspring, even physically fighting men on two occasions to support her older sons in disputes. Her sons were allegedly no angels; though they were never criminally convicted, they were under community scrutiny, as they had been fingered in crimes ranging from shooting to intent to rape. However, they were spared criminal investigation due to their fathers' influence as associates of the Don. Sadie was therefore as loved and respected as she was feared.

Sophia fell asleep on the couch for just over an hour and was awakened by the soft ringing of her cell phone on the side table. "Hello?" she answered drowsily.

"It's your madda," said Sadie in her characteristically strident yet warm voice, which immediately brought her fourth-born wide awake. The camaraderie among Sadie's children and their dominant mother was renowned not only in Tivoli Gardens but also affiliated and oppositional communities alike. The three girls were best friends; they had only separated because Kadia, the firstborn, was at Bethlehem Teachers' College in St. Elizabeth, and Maureen, the second daughter but third child, was invited by her godmother to spend six months in the USA. Kadia was unable to progress to college after high school despite passing all her subjects, due to lack of money. People in the community always remarked that Miss Sadie's girls had not succumbed to the scourge of teenage parenthood; Sophia was the first to break that record, and this caused her some guilt and shame. The boys were all in high school and, under their mother's hawk eye, were apparently staying out of trouble but leading a double or perhaps triple life due to the numerous temptations around them.

Before her mother could start on the subject of Steve, Sophia blurted out, "Mama, is what happen with Dudus?"

"Mi chile, mi just pass through the market on my way here and it look like people can't talk bout anything else." Her enlarged eyes betrayed her inner excitement at the mounting tension in the community. "Dem say de man dem ago barricade up di community 'gainst the police. I don't like the vibes. No, mi daughter, it don't look so good at all."

Sophia was momentarily silenced by the news; she was fourteen when the last such standoff with the police had ended in numerous deaths and injuries of local residents, and she could only shudder at the thought of a recurrence. However, she was also so distressed by her personal troubles that she felt more intensely burdened than she normally would have been by the prospect of a confrontation between the security forces and local strong men.

"Dem say dat outas man dem coming fi help defend the community," Sadie continued. "Dem say Dudus offer dem big money to come help to put up a strong defense against the beast dem."

"But dat sound serious," Sophia responded, adding, "but why dem think that dem need outside help?"

"Dem say this is too big fi di man dem in here," Sadie continued, lowering her voice to a confidential whisper to guard against eavesdroppers who could overhear her on the other side of the thin walls. "It look like the government bringing in the army, and some people even a say dem ask America fi help."

This last revelation momentarily pulled Sophia out of her paroxysms of self-pity as she contemplated the potentially dire outcome of this array of resistance against the local regime of badness.

"It look like Bruce serious," she said, referring to Prime Minister Golding, who was the community's Member of Parliament. "How can an MP turn against his own community though, Mama?" The young expectant mother's musing aloud was as much rhetorical as it was an appeal to stimulate further grapevine revelations from her knowledgeable mother.

Obligingly, Sadie continued in her conspiratorial whisper, "Dem say Dudus have too much secret fi di whole a dem, so that's why him a give up di boss to the farina dem. Mi think you better pack up you tings and come with me outa Old Harbour."

This last suggestion took Sophia by surprise, as leaving Tivoli was the furthest thing from her mind. She was too attached to her routine in town to even consider that suggestion seriously and said so, concluding her protest with, "Old Harbour too dead, Mama."

"A word to the wise is sufficient," replied her mother. "Ah doan want to have to come fi you if things really get hot."

Sophia was silent for a moment, contemplating that possibility, but almost immediately dismissed the suggestion with an appeal to her mother to consider how difficult it would be for her to get to a hospital if her baby came early. "I just have two more weeks to go, Mama. So if you just stay with me till then, I will come and stay with you after the baby born."

Sadie gave her a long, hard look and reached over and pulled up her daughter's dress to reveal her protruding stomach.

"You near fi true," she conceded, running experienced hands over the entire surface of her daughter's belly and feeling the fetus inside move in response. "It look like you can drop any day now. This is a hard decision for me to make because I think this time the community really in big danger. But is true that vehicle hard to get from where mi living outside of the Old Harbour town, and you already register at Jubilee, so maybe we can batter it out here in case a anything, for the sake a di baby."

With that, Sadie got up off the couch and walked the short distance to the refrigerator, which she opened and closed in quick succession.

"Kiss mi neck, Sophia, but you nah eat. You fridge is as empty as a courtroom pon Sunday. You intend to starve mi grandchild before it born? Mi haffi get you some real food fi mek sure dat should in case we have to batten down, you no dead fi hungry.

This motherly criticism provided the opening Sophia needed to explain to Sadie just how desperate her material circumstances were. This brought maternal remonstrations from the worldly-wise Sadie.

"Ah tell you from you tek up wid dat wutliss man him no have no ambition. How you fi a breed fi a man who a work who don't give you anything and him know that you not working or hustling yourself? Dem say pickney a poor people riches but good God, you no have three already?"

Seeing the ready tears well up in Sophia's eyes and roll down her cheeks as this unabashed criticism stung home, Sadie immediately regretted her outburst and reached out to give her daughter a hug.

"All right, all right, done now," she cajoled. "But right now, you need some good chicken foot soup. A going down to Mr. Henry shop to get some meat kind fi go wid dem tings ya," she offered, poking into the market bag. "You have flour and dem ting deh?"

Sophia shook her head, choking back more tears as she whispered, "Mi woulda have more money fi go market this morning, but mi did haffi change mi weave and do mi nails fi go a di dance last night." As she uttered the explanation, she realized she had made a tactical error.

A cloud crossed Sadie's face and exploded in her eyes as she disregarded the proximal dwellers and almost shouted, "Oonoo an dis blasted hear weaving and fingernail! If it was for me alone, dem hairdresser and nail technician deh woulda dead fi hungry. Massa God give oonoo good, good hair and fingernail, an all onoo can tink bout is fi go waste money a paste in hair and paste on fingernail every week dat God send fi go a dance while onoo pickney dem a starve. By the way, a whey di pickney dem deh?"

"Dem down a Marcia," Sophia responded.

Sadie quietly considered what else to say. She was used to her grandchildren's absence, as they often stayed with their cousins, especially when Sophia went partying. Now all teenagers, the three girls were model children, well behaved and doing well in school, despite never having met their respective fathers. They followed the same pattern Steve did, of deserting Sophia when she needed them most, while she was pregnant.

"You have anyone who can come and stay with you right now?"

Sophia hesitated a moment, then slowly shook her head.

"You know I have to go and come," Sadie said, "and I would ask my neighbor Michelle to come and stay with you, but she just did operation last week. She cut a growth in her womb, and she can't walk or stand up strong right now. But you need to have someone to stay when I am not here with you."

"To tell you the truth, Mama, I would ask Junior—"

Sadie did not allow her to finish and cut her off, saying sharply, "Don't call that battyman name to me! I tell you, you going to make people stone you one of these days because you won't stop associating with that faggot."

"I know you don't like Junior, Mama, but over the years, he was one person I could always rely on to help me out. He used to help me with the children, like you wouldn't believe, braid their hair, tidy up the place, cook food. He even used to go market, but he has not gone there from last year since they beat him up. But I think that was really unfair because whole heap of the vendors who have stall are faggots, and nuff battyman inna the society too, all the bigger heads. So is why them choose to beat up Junior and not them?

"Anyway," Sophia went on, "Me myself got into problem with him from the other day because he come and tidy up the place good, good, good, till I could not even find some of my own things. When I called him to ask him about the expensive cologne that was on the dresser, which is the one thing mi have to show that Steve was here, he claimed he never saw it. Well, Mama, that was when I realize that him both lie and tief! So I cuss him dog rotten that even fass Marcia knock pon mi door to ask me what a gwaan! Him shame the day, and I don't see or hear from him since that. But me a tell you the truth dat God love. If it was for the battyman ting alone, mi wouldn't mind him because you same one teach we to love everybody doan? But a tief and a liar mi can't abide, no time at all."

"Serve you right, is all I can say," Sadie responded tartly. "If you can't hear then you will feel."

They were both silent for some moments, then Sadie laughed and said ruefully, "If you were not such a war boat, you wouldn't have cut yourself off from all your old friends."

"Mama, to tell you the truth, I feel better off without all those hypocrites and parasites," Sophia retorted. "All and all some of them want is to know your business so they can spread it. Right now, if a person naw come genuine, dem can galang."

"You are too young to be so bitter in your heart, seriously," Sadie said, softening her tone considerably. "But you remind me of myself when I was your age in so many ways. It is very hard, though, to go through life alone. Sometimes you have to see and blind and hear and deaf. But all this don't solve the problem. It seems like against my better judgment I am going to have to stay here at least for the next two weeks with you till you have baby, police or no police. I just hope it don't get too drastic.

Hear what. I am going to go now and buy the chicken foot and some other things and come back and make the soup. You better call the girls and tell them you are home so at least they can come and keep you company."

"Mama, ahm…" Sophia faltered because she knew she was going to put her mother under more pressure, but she had no recourse really. "I don't have anything to take with me to the hospital for the baby."

"What?" Sadie spluttered. "That wutliss boy don't give you anything. No sah, mi nah mek him get way with this. He is working, so he will have to stand up like a man. After a no dog get you pregnant! Come on! Dial him right now and make me give him a piece of mi mind!"

There was no denying Sadie what she wanted when she wanted it. She was born under the sign of Leo, and she made no bones about being a leader, especially where her offspring was concerned. Sophia dialed Steve's number, and when he came on the phone, she restrained her instinct to spit fire at him and instead asked coolly, "How are you?" As she expected, her tactic disarmed Steve, who, like many others, branded her as quarrelsome without also appreciating her more sensitive side.

"All right," he managed to croak, and before he got a chance to compose himself fully for what he expected would be an onslaught from Sophia, the mother of his unborn child stunned him further by saying, "Sadie wants to talk to you, Steve."

By now, Sophia had turned the speaker up on her phone, so both she and Sadie heard quite clearly Steve's sharp intake of breath at this announcement. The real onslaught was coming as he'd anticipated but from an unexpected source!

Sadie's voice penetrated deep into Steve's psyche as she said with deadly quiet, "What do you expect, that you are going to treat this like you are some stud and Sophia is some slave on massa plantation? You need to wake up and smell the coffee. If you think and believe you are going to abandon her when she need the help most, you make a simple and sad mistake. And I am not talking about you giving her cocky because if you show up here with that little ding-dong, I am going to castrate you myself. But you better bring some money. Her time is near and is not like in my days when you could wrap baby into any and anything. Right now, it's all about Pampers, receiver and dem ting deh and dem ting deh cost dollars. So, by Friday, you have to come up with fifty grand, and I will call you when we need to get some more."

Steve had always been a little afraid of Sadie. She was his idea of a true matriarch. He felt cold sweat washing him and had difficulty holding the phone in hands that had suddenly become quite slippery. He finally found his voice, although it seemed determined to play tricks on him, cracking unexpectedly mid-sentence. "I can't manage the fifty grand right now, Sadie. I will give you twenty when I get pay end of month."

On the other side of the conversation, Sadie winked and smiled broadly at her offspring, although her voice was suitably harsh as she replied, "You just make sure of that, you know, or else mi a go deal wid you misself!" And with that parting shot, she disconnected the call, leaving a bemused Steve to recover his composure as best he could.

"You must know who to war with, Sophia," Sadie said with a twinkle in her eyes. "You can't pet man nowadays when them a gwaan like asshole. You have to tek di fight to them. Just remind me when payday a come so mi can tun up di pressure pon him."

Sophia looked at her mother with renewed admiration and shook her head in lingering disbelief at Steve's ready acquiescence to Sadie. "If it was me, he would be full of excuses, you know. I never met a man as mean as Steve. Before him give me anything, he tell all kinds of lies. As far as I am concerned, he never have money yet."

"I am going to be his worst nightmare…bright! I am going to make him know how water walk go a pumpkin belly," Sadie replied with a chuckle. "Call Kemesha and tell her its time she, Kaylia, and Tamara find dem backside back here now because the whole place waan clean. A whey so much dust come from? Mi can just imagine say a pure cable dem down a Charmaine and dem a watch. No badda get up," she said as Sophia tried to lumber her heavy body out of the settee. "You try and keep your legs up. Bout you gone a Passa Passa last night. I feel it in my bones, though. It is going to be a rass and a rasshole in this community before too long."

With that, Sadie Baynes let herself out of her daughter's apartment and headed down the stairs and into the street toward Mr. Henry's shop, thinking as she went how her daughter's misfortunes were umbilically tied to her use of her body and not her head in trying to hold a man. "And is as if she can't see, don't know about pill and condom and nuh have no strength for man," she muttered out loud. This reflection spun her, inevitably, back into the corridors of the past, and she remembered, as if it were yesterday, the day the three young men had come for Sophia, when she was only thirteen, to say she had been "requested" by the area leader because "her time had come."

The spokesman for the group had deliberately raised his shirt to display the gun lurking in his waistband to emphasize the seriousness of the request. Sadie still could not forgive herself for not having resisted with her life. In her private moments, she could not escape the even more heinous crime, in her own eyes, for having accepted the envelope of money he thrust in her apron before they disappeared with her daughter, whose silent, accusatory tears had streamed down her cheeks. Right after that, Sadie sent the other two daughters off to her mother in Priory in St. Ann; they never came back to the community and now lived with their aunt down the road.

To compensate for keeping Sophia in the community where she watched her spoil herself by adopting social habits that she herself abhorred, Sadie often went out of her way to help her, and this time was no exception. She felt a sort of relief to be going to see Henry, who had been her lover at the time. However, she had also been married to Bernard John, popularly called Blood, who had since been killed by police under questionable circumstances. Talking to Henry, she thought, would give her a chance for an outpouring, which she was rarely able to do because she was so often preoccupied with maintaining her business with her stall and taking care of other people's problems.

As she stepped off the curb and entered the shop, the familiar voice greeted her with as much enthusiasm as ever. Henry maintained he was the man for her and that she should never have left him, but he bore no grudge toward her and was always willing to give her a listening ear.

"Sadie Baynes, a some a di something you carry come give me?" Henry laughed heartily at his own joke.

"Francis Henry, you nuh hear mi say mi surrender the things of the flesh and turn over my life to the Lord?"

"Talk you a talk, Sadie. You never hear what Beenie Man say about the wickedest slam?"

"Cho Francis, man, a serious ting mi come to talk to you about," said Sadie, refusing to be drawn by the unrepentant banter, which was one of the features that had attracted her to him so many years ago. "I want to talk to you about Sophia."

A cloud immediately descended on Francis Henry's forehead, and the smiles vanished from his lips and eyes. "That is the one writ that I have against you, you know, Sadie—that you give away mi pickney to a next man you know. You should have left your husband and call my name on that child."

"Hush, nuh! Suppose someone should hear you?" Sadie cautioned. "I am going to have to come and stay with her till she have the baby because with them a look for Dudus, any card can play, and she need to have someone on spot in case she has to go to hospital."

"Well, at least that sounds good," Henry responded. "That girl get a raw deal from beginning to end. Her self-esteem deh below her foot bottom. You no see how she bleach out her face? And this everlasting hair that she always have to have in and she naw work. You nuh see that she a sell her soul to say nothing about her body for vanity. And a mussi trump change she a collect to cause she always bruk and her pickney dem live pon bag juice and always hungry, a the truth mi a tell you.

"Sometimes when them come fi trust something mi end up put extra things inna the bag because mi know what me know. But you shouldn't have robbed me of that child. Because at least I could have defended it when the Don did send for her. Is true you wouldn't know how that thing cut me up, especially for the fact that I had to keep quiet and gwaan like it don't concern me when I did know it was my flesh and blood. But at least out of the three man dem that use her, two dead and one gone to prison, so it kind of ease off some of that agony."

"It affected her deeper than we realized, you know," Sadie responded. "If you look closer, in every one of her relationships, her pattern is to repeat the abuse and to tolerate some kinds of foolishness from man. At the same time, among women, she has a reputation for being a name-brand war boat to the extent she don't even have one God-almighty-friend she could count on to go with her to lying-in, you see me?"

"Mi see you fi true, that no really sound too right," Henry drawled. "But me never know you turn family counselor, Sadie. All right! Nuh badda lose you cool! You know we just have to take bad sinting mek laugh, you know, tek kin teet kibba heart bun."

"I don't rightly know what to do to fix her business Henry," Sadie still sounded troubled. But I will talk to you some more because I am going to be here for a few days. Sell me four pounds of chicken back, four pounds of chicken foot, two pounds each of cornmeal, flour, and sugar, and a hardo bread. Then what you think going to happen with this Dudus business?"

"Well, that section is politics," Henry lowered his voice significantly. "This time, it serious because mi never see Labourite move 'gainst Labourite yet. I don't really count the time that Seaga gave the list of names to the police because nothing really did come out of that.

"Maybe if the police had taken it serious when Seaga told them Dudus was one man going to give them trouble and they had put some action on that, what is happening could have been avoided. This time, something more serious a gwaan because the Manatt inquiry is something that the whole world was watching, and when Cowboy called Mr. B. a liar, mi think him decide to tek revenge, and ah feel the whole community going to suffer for it."

"Same thing mi say too," was Sadie's rejoinder. "Dog nyam wi supper. Remind me of your number. Ah feel I am going to need it."

After exchanging cell phone numbers, the old couple parted, and Sadie headed back to her daughter's apartment.

Chapter Three

As the dawn skies lightened and the twittering of the birds changed tenor, early risers in Jamaica, from country to town, woke with great anticipation. Everyone was hoping there would be a breakthrough in the standoff between the security forces and the armed men hell-bent on resisting the takeover of Tivoli Gardens by the lawmen. The romantic at heart were hoping against hope that Dudus would not be caught. This sentiment was expressed strongest by those who benefited most from his bounty. They were not too concerned about the moral and legal questions that surrounded his wealth.

On the other hand, political pundits for whom he had performed devious favors were anxious to get rid of him. The diabolical question they asked themselves and one another was "how and when?" The extradition request had therefore come as both a blessing and a curse. It provided the excuse to pull the plug on a don who the powers-that-be thought had become too big for his boots. However, because Coke controlled the voters, and Tivoli Gardens was the center of a prime government constituency, he had to be handled with care.

41

On the Thursday morning that the police broke up the Passa Passa dancehall session, Tivoli Gardens residents woke to the sounds of helicopters droning overhead and intermittent gunfire. As on previous occasions, gunmen had secured the community with barricades to prevent the security forces from entering. What they did not bargain for was that the police would get reinforcement from the army and such great force would be arrayed against them. The seven o'clock news on both television and radio stations conveyed that a curfew had been imposed on the West Kingston area from dawn to dusk to enable the security forces to monitor the movements of those entering and leaving the area. It was totally unexpected. Children had examinations to sit, and workers had duties to attend to, but all that faded into the background. As the newscasters emphasized, the priority now was to catch Coke, since the government in an overnight move had decided to turn the don over to the US authorities. According to police press releases, gunmen were no match for the law officers.

By nightfall, the anxiety that had set in during the day, when citizens realized they were virtual prisoners, was mounting by leaps and bounds for those trapped in the community. No one trusted the offer the authorities had made for residents to leave in buses provided. Adding to the tension, the onset of a general power cut from three-thirty in the afternoon, which was designed to provide cover for the movements of the security forces when darkness fell, caused increased apprehension as citizens worried about the fate of the perishables in refrigerators as well as their own capacity to stay safe from criminal elements and security forces alike. Cell phones were abuzz with concerned inquiries about the whereabouts and state of health of loved ones.

On the third floor of Building Four in a two-room apartment, Bishop Conroy Walters, Head of the New Pentecostal Church of God located on Bayonet Street, checked the time on the clock hanging over his bed. It was six p.m. exactly. Normally on a Thursday evening at this time, the elders of the church would meet at his house for a prayer session. However, because he had not anticipated the power cut, he was caught off-guard when he realized his phone battery had discharged and there was no way to contact the other five persons in the circle. He wondered what the others were doing at that moment. Fortunately, Bishop Walters had a battery-operated radio, and this he now turned on so he could hear the latest news. It was already in progress.

"...two men were reportedly shot and killed in the security operation mounted by the joint security forces in the Tivoli Gardens community in a bid to capture strong man Christopher 'Dudus' Coke," the newscaster was saying. *"The operation, which started at six o'clock this morning and which has intensified during the day with a cover of darkness being facilitated by a Jamaica Public Service endorsed power cut, has resulted in clashes*

between gunmen defending the Tivoli Gardens community behind barricades and security personnel systematically dismantling these barriers. One soldier received a minor injury from a glancing shot to his left ear."

The pastor was interrupted by insistent knocking on his door. Carrying the radio in his left hand and his Bible in the other, he tiptoed to the door and looked through the peephole. Satisfied it was three of his five brethren, Elder Brown, Elder Thompson, and Elder Standard, all of whom lived in the adjacent building, he opened the door and, once they had entered, hastily closed it and turned the key twice to lock it. The three brothers greeted each other with warm hugs, relieved to confirm one another's safety.

Elder Standard explained that the other two—Elders Gibson and Jackson—had been in touch by phone, and apart from being unable to go to Coronation Market for their usual Thursday evening shopping, they were all right. However, they would not be coming over as they all had young children, who were terrified due to the charged atmosphere. They felt it was better for them to stay home.

After leading his brethren through prayer, Bishop Walters fell silent for a while, contemplating the trio with a somber expression. He offered them water, served from the kitchen tap, and they settled around the four-seater table, which was also in the sparse kitchen. The natural light was fading fast, so the bishop lit a candle. Although they were no strangers to gunshots, they flinched every time a gun barked; the explosions sounded unnervingly close. Finally, the bishop spoke.

"As we know, where two or three are gathered, He is in the midst to bless and do us good. These are terrible times we are living in, my friends, and we are in this for the long haul. But at least we have our faith. Without faith, the world at large and we in this community would be at a loss. As devious as some religious institutions are, the moral and spiritual fiber of this society has been maintained by the widespread influence of religious ideology on peoples' ways of viewing the world and responding to situations like this. Thank God that we have used our faith to spread the word of Peace and Love in this community. That should be a big help in this time of trouble. We have not neglected the feeding of the flock.

"So, although some atheists are able to maintain a high moral standard due to their faithfulness to ethical codes that are independent of religion, the masses are more dependent on the Church for resolving their fears, defining their faith, and ordering their spirituality. Many people seek refuge in the religious environment for rituals like christenings, marriages, and burials, and it is customary for one to swear on the Holy Book in courts in the pursuit of justice. But how many people do you think are calling upon God to help them walk through this time without fear?"

Having posed the question, the bishop paused; there was nothing he liked more than a good metaphysical debate. Sensing this, his colleagues entered the discussion right on cue.

Clearing his throat, Elder Standard, who had also studied at the United Theological College and prided himself on being some measure of a philosopher, said, "Social power is usually divided between Church and State. This influence is challenged, though, by the popular culture, which offers major competition to capture the conscience of human beings, especially the youth. The youth are under pressure to reject both Church and State, which by and large have failed to help them and give them hope. Our duty now is to find ways and means to meet the youth halfway. Why do you think they take up guns and are even now defending a man who we all know has done illegal things in his time?"

As if in response to Elder Standard's rhetorical query, a volley of shots rang out, causing all four men to jump. Elder Thompson even ducked. "That was close," he said, visibly shaken.

"They were outside before. They are in the community now," Bishop Walters responded, rising to close the windows and draw the curtains. He replaced the burned-out candle with a fresh one; the wind through the open window had caused it to burn low prematurely.

"We have to be strong now more than ever," he said. "Some of us will not survive this night. I think you had better stay here."

The others agreed, and Elder Standard took out his cell phone and made calls to family members on behalf of the other two since he was the only one who had credit left.

Trying to sound cheerful, Elder Gibson asked the bishop whether he could not "run a boat."

"I have the mind, but I don't have the behind!" The bishop said. "But if you want crackers and cheese and some mint tea, we can have communion." His companions welcomed the suggestion, and he quickly provided the simple fare. As they were eating the bishop became serious once again.

"All of a sudden, I know what it must have felt like when Jesus and the disciples had the last supper. And although I am concerned about what might happen to your families in your absence, I am glad you are here to watch with me in this hour."

The others shared his sentiment, and Elder Gibson noted that at least they all lived with extended family members while the bishop lived alone.

"And we have able-bodied men there with the women in case anything happens," Elder Thompson added.

The bishop pondered a moment, then said, "Ever since Gladys left and took the children, I have not been the same. She could not forgive me for losing all that money in Cash Plus and Olint. I mean, brethren, she almost killed me one night in her anger. I repented and begged her forgiveness, but she stood her ground. She said as the head of the Church I should have known better…" His sentence trailed off as again, double staccato shots rang out simultaneously from opposite sides of the community.

Elder Thompson seemed to forget his religious persuasion for a moment and ejaculated, "Rhatid! Di police bwoy dem a put it on pon dem fi real!"

Following idiomatic suit, the bishop, also code switching, asked, "How you know dat?"

"You can tell the difference with the bwoy dem Chiney K and the police dem AK 47. Although is the same brand, is different maker, so dem sound different."

When silence resumed, it took a while before the four churchmen composed themselves sufficiently to contemplate their interrupted conversation. The bishop took the lead.

"You know, brethren, what we have here is a sure display of the laws of the jungle. Power over the barrel of a gun. The dominant are exercising power over the dominated, and the dominated are exercising their own authority, both refusing to reason and, of course, both disowning the authority of the Almighty. Politics has also been used to enforce the power of the few over the masses, and now the few of the masses are fighting back.

"Because they believe in nothing but acquiring personal power, it is futile and only shows the depth of ignorance informing their behavior—on both sides. Politicians use power to secure mass compliance and order society. To compensate for their powerlessness, the gunmen control the community using fear tactics, and in between these extremes, the security forces are the loose cannons. Although they represent the state, they act as if they are a law unto themselves, and we the citizens are at risk from them all.

"So here we are, huddling and wondering what is going to happen next. Will the gunmen get us or will the security forces? And does the government care? Have they left us to the mercy of the security forces and the gunmen? Who can we depend on to defend us? All we can do is hold on to our faith and pray that the Almighty who sees and knows all will keep us safe from harm, danger, accident, and trouble."

The soberness of his mood was contagious; Elder Thompson had resumed his humble stance during this offering, and his mood was equally contemplative.

"Bishop and brethren, in case I do not survive this, tell my children this for me. The one thing to fear in this world is fear itself, for the fear that humans have developed for the unknown, especially pertaining to life, death, and the afterlife, is futile. This is particularly important in today's Jamaica, in view of the rampant violence. I never knew I would live to see the generation of vipers, but these are the perilous times that the Bible predicted would come in the last days."

"Cheer up, Brother Thompson," Elder Standard boomed. "We are going to survive this like how we survived everything else. Those of us who live in inner-city communities can take it more than most, although this time around, it feels like it is getting harder to bear. These multiple forms and almost continuous incidents of trauma have created personal and social horror and led many to either abandon their faith in conclusion that God cares less for them than for other communities or else encouraged a closer relationship with the sacred realm as a desperate strategy of spiritual survival."

The bishop was about to respond but was cut short by another deafening barrage of shots that seemed now to be coming from the street outside the building.

"I think we should barricade ourselves in, in case of anything," he managed to say before another round followed by loud screams coming from the floor downstairs made them literally bolt for the bedroom.

Chapter Four

THE COMBINATION OF noises in the two-room house was graduating to a pitch that was more intense than usual. The children were unable to attend school because of the curfew in the community, which was now in its second day, and the confinement was making everyone antsy. Kwame, who at seventeen years was the eldest of the four children, was impatient of the boisterous cavorting of his siblings—Andy, aged twelve, Carol, aged nine, and Vivian, aged eight—which was too juvenile for his liking. He took one look at them throwing pillows at each other in the room they all shared and retreated onto the small verandah at the back of the house to do his homework. He was happy he had completed the math assignment before he left school on Tuesday because it was impossible to concentrate on Calculus in this environment.

It was not easy to do, but he pushed the intermittent waves of gunfire washing over the community into the background of his mind and focused on the task of writing the essay assigned by Ms. Henry, the Religious Education teacher. Each student was to critique an aspect of the conflict raging in Jamaica between atheists and Christians. Kwame chose to argue that while religious faith provided a source of social security, it also impeded the process of development, as it reinforced low self-esteem and made believers vulnerable to domination. He cited the case of Africans enslaved in the West to show that the blind religious devotion encouraged by missionaries during the colonial era was an obstacle to rebellion. He also suggested that, like the atheists proposed, the Church was responsible for financially exploiting their congregations and extracting their labor, which supported other forms of domination.

On the other hand, he supported the Christians' position that without faith, people in general, and those living in urban poverty in particular, would have no source of psychological sustenance. As argued by Bible-believing ardents, holding on to one's faith is one of the few remaining sources of strength available to those who must reconcile their lives to rapidly deteriorating political and social conditions. As one pastor from a Seventh-Day Adventist church explained it, "No matter the religion one chooses, it is important to have a belief system, which provides an alternative hook on which to hang your soul when all around us—our institutions of governance and human rights—are disintegrating."

Kwame, who attended Kingston High School in Fletcher's Land, the community in West Kingston adjoining Tivoli Gardens, was an avid reader, critical thinker, and a member of his school's debating team. English Language and Literature were two of his favorite subjects;

these skills allowed him to fluently consider both sides of the debate as he furiously composed his essay.

His argument was more sympathetic to the position taken by the atheists because his passion for history had disillusioned him about religion's potential to provide the poor with a tool of liberation. Instead, his reading of violent colonial incursions into foreign lands had led him to conclude that charges for such crimes against humanity should be calculated and reparations assigned to the descendants of Africans enslaved in the West no matter how many years had elapsed.

However, to maintain a balanced perspective, he also acknowledged the role of liberation theology as a variation of mainstream religious thinking in enabling the faithful to find comfort in religion. He pointed out that in the Jamaican experience, Paul Bogle and Sam Sharpe are good examples of the use of religion as a tool of both mental and physical emancipation. However, as he clarified, it was unfortunate that Christianity overshadowed many other world religions that provided guidance for everyday life, despite their demonization by Christians. From a human rights perspective, he suggested that agnostics and atheists are not inferior to the religion bearers and should be tolerated. He also recommended that proselytizing should be regarded as a crime against humanity, especially where such efforts are resisted by indigenous populations.

Kwame concluded his essay by saying that until a spirit of respect for difference can be engendered in all social relationships, then anarchy and criminality—commonplace features of world cultures today—were bound to prevail.

As if to echo his sentiments, a loud *badooom!* shattered the afternoon atmosphere. The bazooka-like sound reverberated throughout the entire community, and Kwame even felt it in his chest. He hastily gathered up his writing materials and ran into the room. In reflex action, frequently practiced over time, his siblings had already flung themselves under the bed. Kwame kneeled down and whispered, "It's all right. It sounded close, but that must have been over at Building D, which is two streets away. It sounded as if they blew off a piece of the building."

"When is Mama coming back, Kwame?" asked Vivian. He was visibly shaking. Kwame squeezed his hand.

"She called to say she will stay with Auntie Jennifer in Trench Town until the curfew is lifted because they might arrest her if she is caught on the street." At that announcement, all three youngsters started to cry, and knowing that they were depending on him to be strong, Kwame made a superhuman effort to bite back his own tears.

"Don't worry," he said, "I am going to make some bully beef and rice. But come from under the bed and come in the kitchen with me." Kwame felt tender and protective toward his siblings.

"You think dem going to catch Dudus?" asked Andy. "Him might as well surrender, otherwise it sound like them going to kill off the whole a wi in ya."

"I don't know. Because of the power cut, I have not been able to listen to the news. But wait a minute," Kwame said suddenly. "I can listen on my phone to the radio."

He put his five-subject notebook in his knapsack, which contained a host of pockets housing various items to address his everyday needs. From one pocket, he now extracted his cell phone, which he put on loudspeaker and tuned to one of the popular stations. He was just in time to hear the female continuity announcer saying, *"We interrupt this program to bring a special item of news just in. A spokesman for the joint security operation now underway in the West Kingston community of Tivoli Gardens has reported a major breakthrough. They have captured the unofficial bodyguard of Christopher Coke, popularly known as Dudus, and are now questioning him under tight security at Up Park Camp, the army headquarters.*

"The curfew, which has been in force since yesterday morning, will continue indefinitely until strongman Coke is captured. The security forces' spokesman indicated they are currently engaged in skirmishes with armed men guarding the community and are confident they are close

to capturing Coke himself. Stay tuned for further updates on this developing situation."

"Well, well, well," said Kwame as he turned off the radio. "If they have Bangaman, is just a matter of time before they tell us they have Dudus because you know seh Bangaman naw lef Dudus one inch!"

Kwame turned off the phone and replaced it in its pocket in his knapsack. They all trooped into the kitchen. While the three children sat around the small table, he took two pots off the drainboard, measured water for rice and put it on the stove to boil. He put the saucepan on low fire with some cooking oil then took a cabbage and an onion out of the refrigerator, cut them up and put them to steam-fry. As soon as they were partially cooked, he stirred in the corned beef, and while this simmered, he washed the rice and added it to the boiling water.

Fifteen minutes later, as everyone started eating, another volley of shots rang out in quick succession; it was as if four sets of guns were being fired. This time, the sounds were uncomfortably close, and the deafening chorus continued unabated for about five minutes then tapered off to a dribble. The hungry children were caught between anxiety to fill their empty stomachs and fear which stymied efforts to eat.

Carol whispered hoarsely, "I have to go to the bathroom."

"Me too!" said Andy, and they both rushed out of the kitchen. Luckily, they had two toilets in the small apartment.

Suddenly, unanimous expressions of grief rang out. Women were wailing, men were shouting, and two distinct voices called simultaneously, "Mi get shot!"

"Whooooiiiee! Somebody help me! Whoooiiiiee! Mi a dead ohhhhhiiiiiee!"

The sounds were unmistakably coming from the same building in which the children resided. Panic-stricken, Kwame forced Vivian to eat three bites of the food then grabbed him by the hand and ran to the front room. "Help me put the settee against the door!" he instructed, and his brother quickly complied. He heard one toilet flushing, and Carol soon bounded into the room.

"You hear dat, Kwame? It sound like Marvin get shot." The sound of the other toilet flushing and the water tap running announced Andy's return to the company.

"Is Marvin and Tony Screw voice mi hear a say dem get shot..." His voice trailed off as another volley of shots rang out downstairs on the third floor.

They heard voices shouting, "Whey di boy dem deh? Whey di gun dem deh?" These shouts were followed by sharp thuds that they recognized as blows being administered by gun butts.

More shots were followed by desperate screams as a woman's voice, which they recognized as that of Miss Martha who sold fruits at the primary school gate, saying, "Wha you jus do officer? Wha you jus do? Good God Almighty! Murder! Murder! Dem kill Andray! Lawd God a Heaven! Fire! Destruction and Brimstone! Mi belly! Mi belly! Lawd God! A kill onoo kill mi son?"

"Shut yuh mouth, woman! A harbor you a harbor gunman in yah?"

Another volley of shots rang out, and this time, the sound of glass shattering was accompanied by more uncontrollable wails and screams.

"Onoo come, go under the bed," Kwame ordered the other three. He quickly dashed to the kitchen for the unfinished plates of food as they complied, and he shoved them under the bed, sliding underneath himself so they were all huddled in the confined space. The shots, intermittent shouts, and wails of distress continued for about another fifteen minutes, then relative silence reigned once again. As the children dragged themselves from under the bed, the unmistakable smell of feces rose to meet them; Vivian's bowels had loosened as a reaction to the intense anxiety. Kwame led him to the shower to clean himself up. As the boy was dressing, a pounding was heard on the door.

"Miss Eugenie! Miss Eugenie! Yuh deh in deh? Mi need some help, do!"

Kwame signaled to the children to be quiet and went to the peephole at the front door. Miss Martha was standing alone, tears streaming down her face, her blue dress covered in blood.

"Wait one minute, Miss Martha! Mama not here, but mi a come. Just give me one minute." Kwame pushed the settee from the door and opened it. The elderly woman dashed quickly inside.

"You have anything like Dettol or alcohol?" The desperation in her voice was unmistakable. "And mi need a pan a water. Di officer dem burst the pipe downstairs, and no water naw flow inna di pipe."

"Yes, Miss Martha, we have some bottles of water and some alcohol."

Kwame was about to get the requested items when Miss Martha grabbed his arm.

"Hold on, Kwame, bad feelings a tek me!" And with that, she fainted.

Kwame lowered her onto the couch. "Quick, Carol," he said urgently, "get the bottle of rum from the kitchen table!"

Carol ran to do his bidding. Andy and Vivian hovered, looking anxiously at the froth gathering at the corners of Miss Martha's mouth. Kwame ran for a bottle of water and a towel, which he quickly soaked and wiped the woman's face. When Carol returned with the rum, he poured a little in the cork of the bottle, sapped her face with some, and held the cork under her nose. Soon, her eyes fluttered open. She stared at them uncomprehendingly for a moment before the panic returned and she struggled to a sitting position.

"Quick! Give me the rum and the water! De police dem kill Andray and Mass Tom get shot inna him leg, an mi a go give him likkle help. Whoooiiee, mi belly!" She took the items and fled outside and down the staircase.

Kwame closed the door and said to his siblings, "Eat. I don't know when we are going to eat again. I am going to call Mama to tell her what happened."

Taking the plates from under the bed, he doled them out to the other three, keeping one for himself. They all returned silently to the kitchen, too shocked for words. Kwame reached in his knapsack for his phone and dialed their mother's number.

Chapter Five

WHEN KWAME ENDED the call to his mother, it was four-thirty in the afternoon. Eugenie Carter, the children's single parent, told him she would contact her brother, a police sergeant, to escort her home; she could not bear for them to be on their own in the face of the intense trauma they had experienced since the onset of the curfew in the community. It was five forty-five when the children heard the familiar sound of their mother's key turning in the lock, and they all rushed to the front door to meet her. As she entered the house, Mrs. Carter was engulfed in a four-way bear hug, and the children all started to tell her what had happened.

"Hold on, hold on, one at a time," she said. And from experience, she added, "From youngest to oldest."

They all sat on the couch, and one by one, they related the gruesome tale. When Kwame detailed what had happened with Miss Martha, quick tears sprang to their mother's eyes and trailed down her cheeks. Miss Martha had been Eugenie's friend since childhood, and they had both attended the same dressmaking school. The forty-year-old dressmaker gathered her children close and wept for a while, mingling her tears with her children's. Finally, she inquired whether they had eaten, and when they admitted they had tried to have the meal Kwame had prepared, she did not have the heart to remonstrate with them. Instead, she opened the bag she had brought back and gave them each a bun and cheese sandwich.

"I am going to make some mint tea," she said, "because I don't want gas taking up onoo belly. Then I am going downstairs to check on Miss Martha." So saying, she went to the kitchen and made a pot of sweet peppermint tea, and when it was ready, she called them to the kitchen.

"Now, no matter who knocks on the door, don't open it. Man to man is so unjust, and in these times, you don't know who to trust. I won't be too long, and I will let myself in." She checked in the cupboard where they stored water for emergencies and counted twenty-one bottles. Taking out two, she said, "Just wipe down yourselves and brush your teeth when you are finished eating, and please don't waste the water."

With that, she let herself out.

Quickly descending the open stairway, Eugenie Carter came to Miss Martha's apartment on the third floor and knocked, calling softly, "It's me, Martha. Eugenie." The door opened, and she quickly went inside. Eugenie was shocked to see that Miss Martha was still wearing the bloody dress. She was literally tearing out her hair and did not seem able to stop wringing her hands and crying. On the settee lay the stiffening body of Andray; Miss Martha had tied his big toes together and wrapped a piece of cloth from his chin to his head to keep his jaws intact. Mass Tom lay moaning on a mattress on the floor, his right leg wrapped in cloth torn from a sheet that was lying beside him. Blood seeped from his wound and stained the bandage. Broken glass from the dresser and the television set was everywhere.

"You see all dis, Eugenie? Di police and soldier dem come in ya an you can't believe how dem behave! After dem shot Andray and shoot out the glass out of di dresser and mash up mi TV, dem go next door and kill Tego and Brian, and a so Mass Tom get shot too because him was over dey a shelter. Right now, mi think sey Mumsie lost her mind because we know sey Tego an Brian a no saint, but dem never haffi treat dem so. And Andray give him trouble when him ready, but Lawd God, Eugenie! Him a no gunman! Andray mighta tief, but him a no gunman. Jesus Christ God Almighty, whoooooooieeee! Mi want justice! Wha mi a go do, Eugenie? Wha mi a go do?" the distraught Miss Martha kept wailing over and over.

Eugenie hugged Miss Martha and led her to the bedroom and made her sit on the bed. She rocked her like a baby, muttering, "Nuh Mind, Miss Martha, nuh mind. Just bear up. Bear up. We haffi keep body and soul together." When her friend's sobbing eased, Eugenie told her, "Hold on. I am going to get the water and help you to clean up yourself, Miss Martha. Night a come down, and we have to live this out and be strong."

Eugenie fetched a bottle of water and returned to the bedroom to find Miss Martha stretched out on the bed gazing dazedly up at the ceiling. She kept muttering, "Wha mi a go do, wha mi a go do?"

Eugenie went to the bathroom and returned with a washrag and towel. Easing the soiled dress off her neighbor's listless body, she tidied her, all the time admonishing her to try to think of her own self and the need to calm her nerves so that she could face what was to come. Eugenie found some olive oil on the dresser and opening the Bible on the bedside table, she read Psalm 35 over the open bottle, after which she used it to anoint Miss Martha from head to toe. Miraculously, the traumatized woman was asleep at the end of the ritual. Eugenie gently clothed her in garments she found in the top dresser drawer, covered her with a cool blue sheet, and lay the open Bible beside her head.

Returning to the front room, Eugenie went over to Mass Tom, who was still groaning in pain. "You want anything, Mass Tom?"

"Water, mi daughter, a glass a water. Thirst a kill me."

Eugenie went to the kitchen, took a glass out of the cupboard and wiped it with a towel. She poured water and gave it to the elderly man, who gulped it down in three swallows.

"Mi missis don't even know where me is," he said mournfully. "Mi did only come over here to collect mi partner draw, and because Mumsie never have all of the money, mi was waiting till she get everything when this happen. Me was just in the wrong place at the wrong time. Mi missis mussi a go mad now a wonder whey mi deh." Mass Tom wiped his eyes, which had become moist as he spoke.

"Hold on a little," Eugenie said. "Mi going to see if mi can tek out the shot because you can get lead poisoning if the shot stays in your leg too long. I am going upstairs to get you something to eat and get Kwame to help me, all right? Just hold on."

Eugenie let herself out of the apartment, leaving the night latch on and hurried up the stairway. She let herself in and was surprised to see only Kwame in the front room.

"Whey di other pickney dem deh?" she enquired.

"Sleeping," said Kwame, looking as if he could use some rest himself.

"That is actually a blessing in disguise," said the mother, torn on the inside, though, at the thought of leaving the children on their own but knowing she had no choice in the emergency that had presented itself. As a precaution, however, she woke up Carol and told her that she and Kwame were going to help the neighbors and asked her to make sure if the boys woke up, they would not be alarmed.

"I am going to leave the lamp on in the room and take the candle," she said aloud, "because mi don't want to burn down the house."

Explaining to Kwame what she planned to do, Eugenie, who once before had to remove a shot from a neighbor's son when he clashed with rival gang members, retrieved the first-aid kit, which she had acquired from the Red Cross after that occasion, from the suitcase in the closet. She had hidden it so that the children would not use the supplies without good cause. Arming herself with the kit, two more bottles of water, Dettol antiseptic, the bottle of rum, matches, and two candles, she motioned to her son that she was ready, and they descended the stairs.

Once inside the neighbor's apartment, Eugenie made a cup of instant soup; Mass Tom needed no encouragement to drink it quickly. He moaned in renewed pain when the bandage was removed from the wound, which had stopped bleeding but had swollen considerably. After cleaning the area around the shot entrance, Eugenie took from her handbag the insulin syringe for the diabetes that had plagued her for the past year. She used it to inject some of the rum-soaked marijuana she also kept in a rum flask in her bag, and while she waited for the drug to take effect, she boiled a pair of scissors and a sharp, pointed cutting knife.

"Kwame," she instructed her son, "you have to keep this handkerchief in Mass Tom's mouth in case he feels pain. We don't want him screaming because that might make the officer dem come back. And just hold him because this is not going to be easy."

As added precaution, she gave the old man two tablets from a strip of painkillers. Retrieving the makeshift surgical instruments from the stove, she cleaned them further with a swab of Dettol-soaked gauze. Testing the mid-thigh area of the wound for pain by pressing in a two-inch diameter, Eugenie asked Mass Tom to tell her if he experienced discomfort.

"It dead, dead, dead, Miss Eugenie. Lawd God a heaven, mi good a lose mi foot to rhatid!"

"Don't worry yourself," Eugenie said soothingly, "you are going to be just fine."

She sanitized her hands carefully, applied a pair of thin rubber gloves and in a swift move made a three-inch-wide incision about an inch deep. Blood spurted onto the sheet she had wrapped under Mass Tom's leg.

Mass Tom's eyes were shut tight, but Kwame felt his stomach contract at the sight of the profuse flow of blood. It was the closest he had come to the raw evidence of the violence stalking his community, and he could not stop his hands holding Mass Tom from trembling.

Noticing this, Eugenie said softly, "Don't worry, my son, this won't take long."

She used her forefinger to probe the opening she had created, and after ten seconds, she made a sharp intake of breath when she felt the hard, embedded object. She cut down a further quarter inch and eased out the bullet, which she cleaned and carefully wrapped in gauze. Staunching the flow of blood with a thick wad of gauze, she then used the threaded needle she had earlier prepared and quickly stitched the wound. Mass Tom did not open his eyes until she had cleaned and bandaged the cut, which, mercifully, was still benefiting from the injection.

"You can open your eyes now, Mass Tom, and look at the evidence," Eugenie said. The old man slowly complied.

"We are going to use this to nail dem bastard deh to the cross." She indicated the gauze-covered bullet. "I will keep it safe and sound. Do you have a phone number for your missis?" she asked as an afterthought.

"No, but mi have a number fi mi granddaughter who deh a di house. A mussi Massa God works because when me a lef the house yesterday, she write it down pon piece a paper and give it to me." Rummaging in his shirt pocket,

Mass Tom retrieved a carefully folded piece of paper with the number written on it.

Eugenie took her phone from the back pocket of her jeans and made the call right away. The mutual relief at the communication breakthrough was tangible.

As she ended the call, Eugenie concurred with Mass Tom's earlier admonition, saying, "Yes, God naw sleep, you see it too," adding, "Look, mi a go make a cup a tea fi yuh, and yuh drink it and try get some sleep—"

"Nuh trouble yourself bout tea, Miss Eugenie, God already a go bless you for the work what you do today. Just give me another glass of water, and mi will lie down right ya so and go sleep. One thing, though. Mi want fi make some water inna the toilet first," he added with a rueful chuckle.

Both Eugenie and Kwame lifted him and carried him to the toilet.

"Is a good thing dat you so mawga, Mass Tom," said Kwame, "otherwise we couldn't manage to carry you!"

Kwame assisted the elder to urinate, and they returned him to the mattress. After drinking the water, Mass Tom settled himself under the sheet Eugenie found in the dresser drawer; it was not long before he was snoring. After cleaning up the area, securing the first-aid kit and collecting the empty bottles, Eugenie left the night latch on and secured the door using a piece of cardboard she tore off the edge of a box in the kitchen. Wearily, she and Kwame headed back up the stairway to their apartment and flopped onto the couch.

Kwame was just about to doze off while Eugenie was looking in on the sleeping children when deafening gunshots rang out once again. The children woke up instantly, as the explosions seemed to come from every angle of the community. Kwame grabbed his knapsack and turned on his phone radio to catch the news update. Mother and children looked at one another in consternation at the announcer's statement, which rose over the din.

"We repeat the news flash just in. The security operation personnel are now in Tivoli Gardens in full force and are engaged in pitched battle with the gunmen who have sworn allegiance to the fugitive, Christopher Dudus Coke. Numerous casualties have been reported and the confrontation seems set to continue."

"Mama, wha we a go do?" asked Andy in obvious terror.

"Mi no know, mi no know," she said tightly as she and Kwame shoved the couch behind the front door. They all moved into the bedroom, and after securing the door with a bolt, they all huddled together under the queen-size bed, putting pillows over their ears to muffle the deafening blasts that sounded similar to what they remembered from watching the invasion of Iraq on television.

Chapter Six

F RIDAY NIGHT PROVED to be one of the longest in the living memories of the Tivoli Gardens residents. As the gunfire intensified and residents detected both the high-pitched whine when bullets bounced off walls as well as the hollow sounds of shots connecting with flesh, it was impossible for young or old to find comfort in rest when a cacophony of grief accompanied the onslaught. Cries from the wounded mingled with anguished wails from relatives, friends, and strangers alike. Those brave enough to peep into the darkened streets from behind drawn curtains saw troops marching several men at gunpoint into open trucks and driving them away. This set another wave of lamentation in motion. With further shock, residents detected the unmistakable smell of burning flesh, which was familiar from experiences over the years of the fate that sometimes befell those who ended up on the wrong side of murder.

Hearing the explosions, Sadie realized that she, Sophia, and the children may have made the wrong decision to stay in Tivoli Gardens after all. They, like other residents, were not interested in boarding the buses sent by the authorities whom they could not trust to protect them.

There was a general fear that if they abandoned their homes and the community, they might face ridicule and reprisals for being disloyal. Looters were also likely to destroy any property they could not take with them.

In any event, no one expected this level of viciousness from the security forces, and from the weight of the fire power and the strange uniforms reportedly worn by some soldiers, the local forces had outside help.

When she dialed Henry's number and got no response, Sadie felt chilly hands of fear grip her guts, but then she looked at Sophia's sweating face and realized she had an even bigger concern.

"Mama, I feel that my time come," Sophia whispered hoarsely against the background noise of subdued yet steady gunfire.

Sadie's own womb contracted in empathy. She would have to do her best and perform midwife duties because it was a great risk to go outside. She sprang into action as Sophia began to moan.

"Kemesha, take Kaylia and Tamara..." She trailed off as her grandchildren began to cry.

"Mama, we can't go anywhere out there with all that going on." Kaylia, aged fifteen, was trying to sound composed. Tamara, aged eleven, was not even attempting that pretense, while Kemesha, a seventeen-year-old who had seen too much violence for one still so young, remained silent, fingers pressed to her temples as she tried to stave off the characteristic headache that attacked her when she got stressed.

After some time, Kemesha said with maturity, "Do what you have to do, Mama. I think we should go in the other room. I will boil up some water for you and get newspaper and cut up some towels. It's funny—when we talked about this in biology class the other day, I never imagined I would have to be a midwife in real life."

Sadie was duly impressed. Although she had witnessed two births—apart from experiencing her own children's arrivals—she had to admit she was feeling a bit squeamish at the thought of delivering her grandchild. However, now the amnesty period had passed and the buses that had been perched on the edges of the community awaiting those who desired to leave had all departed, the last route of escape had been virtually cut off.

Sadie felt real disquiet when Sophia's water burst and she saw blood. That was not a good sign, and Sadie immediately dialed Donna's number.

Donna was a nurse who lived in the next building. When she came on the phone, Sadie cut to the chase, saying, "Sophia having baby right now and a wonder if you can chance it and walk through the tunnel and come over?"

"Inna the night now, Sadie?" The terror at the prospect was unmistakable in Donna's voice.

"Well, mi no think you can walk on the street with so much gunshot a fire," Sadie responded. "Mi really call you because mi don't rightly know why she have blood in her water."

She heard the sharp intake of breath before Donna said, "It could be breach. You are going to have to be careful that the cord not wrapped around the baby's neck."

Sadie swallowed hard in an effort to move the lump that was growing in her throat, but she didn't succeed.

"So you naw go chance it, Donna?"

"Sadie, a true you mussi doan know wha a gwaan out a road. Di soldier and police dem a round up outa man an man from inna di community and all woman too, and mi no hear bout nobody coming back home. It bad, really bad."

In the next room, Sophia was beginning to groan.

Knowing she had to preserve the credit she had put on her phone, Sadie said, "All right, Donna. May Massa God get we through this!"

Ending the call, the businesslike side of her seemed to take over, and she collected the towel pieces Kemesha had cut up and the bundle of newspapers she had ready. "Where is the hot water?"

"I poured it in a pan and put the Dettol in another pan."

Sadie took a deep breath and picked up a bundle of newspapers from the table in the hallway and headed to Sophia's room where her moaning was noticeably louder, building up against the constant whine of machine gunfire outside, intermittently interrupted by loud *vroom!* sounds, which echoed suspiciously like the mortar fire in war movies.

"Nuh mind, Sophia. Bear up, mi daughter, bear up." Sadie tried to sound soothing as she checked Sophia's dilation. It seemed like two fingers' width; a long way to go before head-crowning ease.

"Mama, mi should really go doctor because the last time, they said this baby going to be extra big, and mi really ketch mi fraid when mi see the blood."

"The baby coming footway," Sadie responded bluntly, and Sophia gasped. "I am going to have to be very careful to make sure the cord don't wrap around 'im—" Sadie's words were cut off by more gunshots as a new commotion erupted in the street below. Shouts of "Murder!" rang out in the hot night air amid the loud wails of female voices, crying, "Help! Help!"

Fear clutched at the strings connecting Sadie's heart to her chest cavity, but she turned back with determination toward her laboring daughter.

Suddenly, there was a banging on the door, followed by shouts of, "Police! Open Up!"

"What the…?" Before Sadie could finish uttering the expletive, a loud explosion signaled they had shot the lock and kicked the door off, and at least nine officers, from Sadie's quick count, burst into Sophia's room. It was beyond the expectations of any high-drama movie director.

"Who and who live here?" one demanded.

"What you mean, who live here? Who you see here is who live here!"

"How you so feisty?" shouted another, young enough to be Sadie's grandson, in unison with a scream from Sophia, whose spread-eagled legs and crowning vagina were at odds with the nervous fidgeting of the intruding officers' trigger fingers.

Sadie turned to the policeman and said haughtily, "A mad oonoo mad or what? Oonoo don't have any respect for life and the sacredness of a woman giving birth? Is like the devil let loose inna oonoo! Begone out of mi daughter house! And may the Lord have mercy on oonoo! We covered under the blood, in Jesus' name, and if you kill we one time, you can't kill we again!"

"How you love chat up you mouth pon big man so?" demanded another officer. "You no 'fraid a police?"

All this time, Sophia was groaning and screaming intermittently as her labor pangs intensified.

"Chat up? Chat up?" By now, Sadie was livid. "But a you coulda bright! Is a great pity dat Massa God didn't give man pussy so that onoo coulda bleed and breed and push out baby like woman. Maybe then you would have respect. Bout who live here! Bright!"

With that parting shot, Sadie turned her back on the officers to give the task of delivering her grandchild her undivided attention. Sophia started to scream as if she were in mortal danger, and Sadie sensed her daughter was exaggerating her pain to create a distraction, thereby reducing the mounting tension in the room because the young, trigger-happy officer seemed ready to snap back a retort.

Sophia herself was wondering whether the officer realized he was behaving like a girl with this tracing attitude, but before she got any further with this thought, the extra screams became real, as a heavy, bearing-down feeling in her birthing canal signaled the baby was on her way out. Sophia took a deep breath and, with a well-timed heave, gave birth to another daughter.

The company of officers were transfixed by what they were witnessing and suddenly seemed self-conscious of the incongruity between their attachment to their death weapons and the life-giving sequence in which they were unwittingly participating.

Not one of the officers had witnessed the entry of a baby into the world before; they were all under twenty-five years of age and were relatively new recruits, so bemused with the power they had acquired that they rarely stopped to critically reflect on the metaphysical dimensions of their existence.

One officer, who was just nineteen and had earlier that night used the butt of his gun to knock a young man unconscious then reacted in like manner when the boy's mother took a potty of stale urine from under a bed and threw it in his face, felt a wave of remorse creeping its way into his psyche. One of his colleagues had shot mother and son in their heads, execution style, as they lay motionless on the floor and hustled him out of the apartment. Now, as he witnessed the birthing, he struggled with a lump in his throat and the tears that unexpectedly stung the back of his eyes. He could not explain why, but he saw a connection between the two incidents, as if God was showing him a sign. He was further convinced of this when his colleague who had fired the fatal shots could not restrain his retching and vomited right where he was standing; the vomit splashed on Sophia's prized red leatherette settee.

Things took an even more surprising turn, however, when Simon Clarke, the officer who had only a few minutes before been acting so aggressively toward Sadie, turned to her and apologized for the intrusion and their generally poor behavior. "If you need any help..." He trailed off, struggling with the contrite character that taken him over.

Sadie didn't know how to take this behavioral shift and busied herself with the process of detaching the placenta from the umbilical cord by deftly measuring two finger joints, as she had seen it done after her own birthings, then cut and knotted it in one smooth action. After cleaning the filmy substance off the baby's body and making sure the nasal passages, ears, and mouth were clear, she finally said somewhat gruffly, "If you want to make yourself useful, tell yuh bredrin dem to clean up ma place and leave. Mr. Mention over there have to clean that vomit off my settee. You can plug in the kettle to make some hot water. Take two of those bottles filled with water, a bucket, bleach, and a rag out of the cupboard under the sink in the kitchen."

With no time to waste on the officers, she slapped the baby's bottom to check her respiratory system was functioning properly.

Turning to hand the newborn to Sophia, she was in the process of saying, "Congratulations…" when she noticed that Sophia was frothing at the mouth. Simultaneously, a heavy gush of blood poured from her daughter's vagina, spraying the bottom of the bed with a stream that was sustained for about five seconds. The officers who had not had a chance to heed Sadie's requests sprang into action and, as of one accord, headed toward the front door, exiting as quickly as they could. All, that was, except for the transformed Officer Clarke, who asked for extra towels to assist Sadie in her efforts to staunch this human hemorrhage.

Given the nature of their mission in the Tivoli Gardens community, Clarke was not surprised by the hasty retreat of his colleagues, yet witnessing Sophia give birth had the opposite effect on him. It had shocked him into realizing they had come to accept inhumane behavior as a norm, and he suddenly felt a bond with Sophia because his own mother had died in childbirth after delivering his younger sister.

"We have to get them to the hospital, somehow," he said, pulling out his cell phone and dialing as he spoke.

Sadie called Kemesha to hold the baby on Sophia's breast while she did what she could to mop up the red tide dripping from her daughter's still-open crotch. She redialed Donna's number and said urgently as soon as she came on the phone, "She is bleeding like a stuck pig. A police officer is here, and he is going to see if they can take her to the hospital. She is frothing—"

"It is a big risk to move her now," Donna interrupted, "but she is going to need blood."

Meanwhile, the officer switched on his phone speaker so Sadie was able to hear a voice coming through against a very noisy background.

"Sarge, emergency, this is Corporal Clarke in charge of Squadron 10. A woman just had a baby and is bleeding to death and needs to go to the hospital."

The sergeant exploded at the other end. "Pregnant woman? Had baby? What are you talking about, man? What you a talk bout woman a have baby? Hospital what? Look nuh! We never come in yah fi pet and powder people. That is no emergency compared to our mission. We are here as agents of the state to get rid of criminal elements, so make her call the man who breed her to carry her to hospital!"

The corporal turned the speaker off, but it was too late for him to protect Sadie from the implications of the sergeant's declarations. He said in a subdued voice, "Copy that, Sir. Following orders."

Taking the baby from Kemesha, Sadie asked her to supervise Kaylia and Tameka to fix breakfast of fried eggs, bread, and cornmeal porridge. She put the baby on her daughter's breast and was heartened to see her weakly embrace her infant. Sadie wiped Sophia's face with a dampened rag and massaged olive oil on her head while repeating the Twenty-third Psalm, after which she prayed in her Warrior style, concluding, "Jesus, stand against the evil that is challenging us inside and outside, oh, Lord God Almighty! May the blood of life prevail over the blood of death! Let your will be done, oh Jesus!"

The officer had no verbal response for this passionate plea for Divine intervention, but he knew from enough encounters with death and dying that when Sophia suddenly opened her eyes and whispered, "Water!" she was on her way out, or as old people would say, she was traveling.

Sadie knew this too and started to slap Sophia's face frantically, pleading, "Don't leave me, my daughter. Don't leave me!"

Corporal Clarke headed to the kitchen, where the girls were silently sitting around the table, the breakfast they had prepared untouched, as they seemed to be in varying stages of shock. "I am sorry for my abusive behavior tonight," he declared to the three of them before collecting a cup from the drainboard and filling it from one of the bottles under the sink. Hastily gulping down the water, he filled the bucket, retrieved the cleaning things as Sadie had instructed and went back to Sophia's room. He knew he was too late when he saw Sadie closing Sophia's eyes with silent tears coursing down her cheeks.

"Mi baby gone, mi baby gone," Sadie moaned. She seemed to have forgotten her newborn granddaughter momentarily.

Clarke picked up the baby and held her awkwardly. "But at least she left you something to hold on to. You know, I don't think I can go back, not after tonight. Mi guilty like the rest, but mi haffi go run 'way. A nuff nuff people get dead tonight. And plenty are not going to be accounted for because who no burn gone bury under cover of darkness."

Corporal Clarke started to tremble as if in a fit of ague, and Sadie had to rescue the baby from his arms. He fell to the floor as his spasms grew stronger, and Sadie could not help thinking he must be really traumatized.

"You know," she said out loud, "The authorities just put onno young people in the force and put a gun inna onnoo hand and tell onnoo fi go shoot people like say oonoo think people is wild animal. How come this supposed to be modern days and better than slavery?"

The young officer did not respond, and it was some time before the violent trembling stopped wracking his body.

"You haffi go find some country to run away to," Sadie told him. "Police work not fit for human consumption. It has turned you into a sick soul."

"Is true, Madda," the officer whispered, repeating, "I can't go back."

Sadie was momentarily at a loss as to what to do. There was no way the undertaker could come into the community under the prevailing siege conditions, and she needed formula to feed the baby. They had overlooked the possibility of Sophia not surviving the birthing. However, now she thought about it, her daughter had put her body under a lot of pressure, going to the dance and climbing all those stairs. Sadie also blamed the Incursion's traumatic conditions for the stress of the home delivery, and now mobility was further compromised by the state of emergency.

When she checked Sophia's neck now, Sadie felt the warmth ebbing away and rigor mortis setting in, so she wrapped a scarf around her chin and knotted it on top of her head, after which she cleared away the blood-soaked towels and removed the stained sheets, bathed her daughter with the Dettol water and dressed her in a blue-and-white track suit she found in the seven-drawer dresser, having taken the precaution to place several sanitary pads in her underwear. She then took one of Kaylia's ribbons to tie her daughter's big toes together and asked the corporal if he could use his authority to get to a shop downtown when daylight broke to get feeding bottles and powdered milk for the baby. He agreed to play this subversive role and asked if he could stay with the household for the rest of the night.

Sadie consented. Under the circumstances, being on their own was a worse fate for her and the girls than being assisted by this renegade cop. For now, the baby was sleeping, and Sadie called the girls to join her in the other room to await daybreak, while Corporal Clarke completed the unfinished task of cleaning the couch, upon which he then lay and promptly fell into the sleep of sheer exhaustion.

Chapter Seven

BY SATURDAY MORNING, the true extent of the crisis was clear. As the rising heat from the sun connected with corpses lying in the streets as well as those resting in the cramped apartments, the unmistakable stench of death assaulted proximal residents. This was a high stage of trauma in the ongoing nightmarish experience.

Fortunately for Brother Ken, a Rastafari Bobo priest who occupied a ground-floor studio apartment in Building A, he was not in the direct line of fire, although, like other residents, he was outraged by the Incursion and its aftermath. His Friday night had been as sleepless as everyone else's, but not a man to linger between the sheets, he rose at his usual five o'clock. As his agile feet hit the floor, he began his daily exercise regimen; sun salutations were smoothly followed by calisthenics, after which he did a Tai Chi routine.

Energized, Brother Ken went to the bathroom, had a cold shower, and brushed his teeth. Looking at his lithe body in the full-length bathroom mirror, he said aloud, "Ol boy, you look damn good for sixty-eight!" He gathered up his floor-length locks and coiled them on top of his head, wrapping them in a white turban. He then covered his body in white pants and shirt and overlaid it all with a flowing white robe; it was Sabbath, and despite the mayhem surrounding him, he was determined not to interrupt his worship ritual.

He could not resist turning on the radio, however, but was certain this exception to his usual rule of shutting out the world on Sabbath was excusable under the circumstances.

"There are conflicting reports of the death count in Tivoli Gardens at this time," the female announcer reported. *"On the one hand, the security forces are reporting that fifty-four persons are confirmed dead. On the other hand, more than eighty persons have called this station with statements of dead or missing relatives. Since both accounts remain unconfirmed, we're emphasizing that at a numerical confirmation of the number of dead or injured in the troubled Tivoli Gardens community would be premature at this time.*

"In further news on the situation, the Jamaica Public Service says it will suspend the temporary power cut in the community between the hours of eight a.m. and five p.m., in order to allow residents to carry out domestic chores. The curfew remains in effect, and only persons employed in the essential services and security personnel are allowed to move about to accommodate minimal movement in and out of the community..."

We are prisoners in our own community, Brother Ken thought as he turned off the news. Looking out of his window confirmed he was not the only one who had been listening to the radio; that or interpersonal communication had spread the reports because the streets, which had been relatively quiet before, were swarming with residents, mainly women. There seemed to be even more police and soldiers than he had observed the day before, who continued to shepherd men with hands on their heads into trucks that were being regularly driven away. From the body language of the guarded processions, Brother Ken had a distinct impression of parallel reality between chain gangs of Africans enslaved in the Americas and the current situation.

The ring of Brother Ken's phone drew his attention away from the sight, and he smiled when he saw the name on the screen.

"Kwame, my son!" he said with joy because he was very fond of his godson. "How are you? How is everyone?"

"We are fine, Brother Ken, but things are not so good with Miss Martha. De police dem kill her son Andray, and Miss Martha well stressed out. Nuff other people over here get shot and some dead, but at least we are alive. Brother Ken, since is Sabbath and dem lift the curfew, can I come over and talk to you personally?"

"How can I refuse you, Kwame? I understand the situation, and the distance is not too far, but let me talk to your mother first."

"I am going to make her call you back because my credit is running out." Kwame hung up.

Shortly afterward, Eugenie came on the line. "Brother Ken, how you do?" After being assured that her cousin and best friend was all right, she continued. "I know it is not far to walk, but I am not sure I want Kwame to come over there with how the security forces behaving so bummy. Moreover, it is Saturday, and you know how much I don't like Saturdays already."

The father of her children had been killed by gunmen holding him up on his way to work at a restaurant on Spanish Town Road one Saturday morning. They had also robbed him of the money he had intended to use to pay down on a secondhand car, his lifelong ambition.

"I don't like how they are taking away so many young men from the community," she added.

"I will come to meet him," Brother Ken said, "and I will bring him back. It is broad daylight now, and people are on the street. Besides, I have some food to give you because I had brought back a whole box of things from country on Monday, and I don't want them to spoil. We don't know if they are going to leave the light on, and there is no time like the present. Don't worry, Sister Eugenie. I will bring him back by three o'clock. I miss my boy, you know."

At this reassurance, Eugenie relented, and Brother Ken quickly left his house.

Meanwhile, the water pressure having been restored due to the work of a local plumber, Kwame took a shower and joined his siblings and mother at the table for mid-morning breakfast. With the exception of Kwame, they all devoured their share of the curried chicken that Eugenie knew was a favorite with the younger children. Of late, Kwame had been requesting vegetarian food; his mother associated this change with his increased closeness to his mentor, Brother Ken. Kwame enjoyed the cornmeal porridge alternative his mother had prepared for him.

"No matter what else you think," Eugenie said, "you are not going to mek Brother Ken turn you into any Rasta. That is what I see shaping up, but that is not going to happen. All and all you going to do is lose your ambition...smoke ganja every day—"

Kwame did not allow her to finish but hugged her and kissed her disarmingly on the forehead. "Whatever I do, I will not let down the side," he said, slinging his knapsack over his shoulder.

"Kwame lucky, eeh?" Carol commented. "You think Mommy would allow me to leave the house now? Even if I was going with a trusted friend, she would say no.

And that will soon go for the two of you." She indicated her brothers. "Only girls suffer from double lockdown."

"At least you are not going far." Their mother sounded as if she was trying to convince herself that her firstborn would be safe. She was unapologetically paranoid; by morning, when her phone started to ring as friends and relatives were able to go out and purchase phone credit, she learned she had lost five close friends and four family members in the Tivoli operation, and her sense of personal trauma was deepening with every passing minute of The Invasion. Even though Brother Ken only lived two lanes away, she felt the familiar churning in her stomach start; this reaction was her inevitable response to gunshots or the threat of danger.

Kwame hugged his brothers and sister, vowing in his heart to treat them more kindly than before, and kissed his mother. He looked through the window, down onto the community street, which had much more human activity than it had during the previous two days. Detecting the unmistakable white-clad figure of Brother Ken coming up the street, he said, "I will go and meet him, Mama, and I promise I will be back in three hours' time. I give you my word."

"All right, son. I will go and look in on Miss Martha and Mass Tom and see what arrangements she going to make to put away Andray. I am taking some of the porridge for them."

"Later!" Kwame called as he left the house and ran down all flights of stairs to the ground. He gave Brother Ken a warm hug.

"Hail up, Brother Ken!" he said, grinning.

"Hurry up and come," Brother Ken rejoined. "No time to waste."

When he arrived at Brother Ken's one-room house, Kwame could hardly wait to launch into the speech that had been building in his head since his essay composition the previous day.

"Brother Ken, I am beginning to believe there is no God. If there was a God, how could he allow us to live in such misery when other people in Jamaica cannot even imagine this kind of existence? How can there be a God when people do not love each other and make guns to kill people just to make money? If there is a God, how come He allows all these things to happen and does nothing about it? How come good is not triumphing over evil in Jamaica or anywhere else in the world?" Breathless, he inhaled sharply, and Brother Ken took the opportunity to offer him a seat and a glass of water.

"Have you eaten, my son?" When Kwame answered affirmatively, Brother Ken reached into a box on the kitchen counter and took out a soursop, which he peeled and placed in a calabash.

"I will eat and listen to you," Brother Ken said, smiling indulgently. "I cannot listen to rantings on an empty stomach."

With that, he settled at the table and ate while Kwame paced the room and continued.

"I mean, I cannot have faith in an unseen Being. Where is the evidence of this faith? What about the evidence of evolution? I am very confused about this angry and jealous God who is going to punish me in hell for thousands of years just because I do not believe in Him— is that kind of tyrant supposed to be someone for me to love? And with all this state of emergency turning every man in this community into a criminal, I am beginning to believe that God only loves rich people and He has no time for the poor. I mean, how can we ever solve our problems?"

Brother Ken sat quietly, listening with great intent to everything his young friend was saying. He studied the impassioned body language as Kwame walked restlessly in the space available in the small room. Even when Kwame stopped speaking, seemingly out of breath and gasping somewhat for air, Brother Ken remained quiet, ruminating on the implications of what he had heard as he finished his fruit, then washed the calabash. Finally, he released his breath sonorously and spoke.

"You have raised some serious issues in that mouthful, Kwame, some serious issues indeed. First, thinking about God does indeed make us question the origins of humankind in terms of Creation and Evolution. Now, the pity is that we are taught to view the world and all objects and relations in it in terms of opposites. We are not taught to explore life in complex terms. Most people in Jamaica only think of a Christian God, and they do not realize how many great religions exist in the world outside this island. Take Buddhism, for example.

"Buddhism teaches us to value our Breath as the source of Life and to use meditation to access a peace of mind. Like the livity of Rastafari, the Buddhists view life in terms of wholeness or an entire way of life that is in harmony with the universe. Proving the existence of God would not be so difficult if people could see that it has to do with how we live with ourselves and one another.

"Now, with Christianity, you are either for the Church or you are against it. This is a very frightening place for young people like you to live, and it is even more dread to consider when we have to live with this kind of tribulation and people uptown don't even know what it is to have soldiers and police treat them worse than dogs. I really hope them catch Dudus and end this soon, but fire and brimstone for all of Babylon and the bigger heads that are all part of the system."

They both looked at each other and fell silent for a few seconds before Kwame spoke again.

"Even if they catch Dudus, I think our problem is much bigger because the politicians that made him and others like him so powerful will continue running things, and none of them will get caught. They will continue to live in their big houses, and we here in the ghetto will still get blamed for everything that goes wrong in the society. And people will still go to church on Sunday and praise God and not question why things are the way they are. That is what makes me so mad." Again, he had to pause to catch his breath.

"The reason Christianity and other religions have such large followings is fear," Brother Ken explained slowly. "People are afraid to question the faith they have been taught. So many wars have been fought because some people were thought to be blaspheming. This is true not only of Christianity, but it also happened with Islam, Hinduism, and even those atheists like communists who feel that religion is the opium of the people as Karl Marx said. They have robbed religion of its capacity to provide a source of sustenance for confused youth, like you, who are too intelligent for mind control, which is really what it amounts to."

Kwame jumped in, saying, "You know, Brother Ken, I think of all this, and I have more questions than answers. Politics in this country is in favor of the rich, and even among the poor you still have man who want to be Don and rule over us. And then the police and soldiers come in and feel they have a right to mistreat us, and there is no one to defend us. Right now, when I saw what they did to Mass Tom...and even Andray and all those other people...did you see the body dem we passed? How long it going to take before undertaker come when dem start to stink up the place already. Gloria even called and told Mommy this morning that dog was eating a body up her lane. So how people supposed to have faith in God when they can't even get justice from mankind? Why is it that it is the poor and the meek who are supposed to inherit the Earth when we cannot even buy food, much less pay rent and buy land? You think they considered how people was going to eat when they cut off the light and everything spoil in the fridge?"

Kwame was so overwrought, he began to cry.

Brother Ken's rejoinder was swift and sharp. "Religion and politics really give us a raw deal my son," he conceded. "Yes, we are taught to view the treasures of the Other world as being more valuable than wealth in the world as we know it." At this point, Brother Ken interrupted himself and smiled at Kwame.

"Well, my son, I am going to see what else there is to eat in my box, and you need to take some for dem other one. In any case, we don't know if the current situation is going to last for long, so you better listen to some music to calm your nerves."

Soon, strains of jazz were coming from the CD player that Brother Ken turned on.

"Who is that?" Kwame asked.

"The great John Coltrane—one of the finest saxophone players that this world has ever seen," replied Brother Ken, taking two ripe plantains and a huge, sweet potato from the box.

Kwame sat at the table and watched his godfather frying them. Although the elderly Rastafari appeared somewhat eccentric because he lived alone and did not mix with people in the community, Kwame found Brother Ken fascinating and had come to appreciate his fine mind, which hosted a spectacular array of thoughts, gleaned from study, travel, and indulgence in myriad social experiences among a vast array of people from different cultures. He did not flaunt his multiple qualifications, but there was no mistaking his brilliance, reflected in his piercing eyes, which seemed to penetrate to one's soul, so steady was his gaze.

Very few persons had ever been in his space and most only briefly. However, Kwame was always welcome, and despite the age difference, Brother Ken treated him like an equal, which had done wonders for his self-confidence. Now, as he waited for the snack, he felt much better than he had done when he first entered the apartment, and for the moment, he suspended his mental anguish and let the soothing music wash over him.

Chapter Eight

I T WAS JUST after four o'clock when Brother Ken locked his front door and prepared to accompany Kwame home. Compared to the previous two days, Saturday was relatively quiet. However, as they rounded the corner of Building B and were heading toward the tower where Kwame and his family lived, a totally different reality greeted them. Women dressed in black with lit candles were walking in circles around four decomposing bodies that lay, wrapped in white sheets, in the street. It seemed this had been going on for some time because a crowd had gathered to watch the ritual.

Brother Ken and Kwame had been so preoccupied with their discussion and musical interlude that the sounds of mourning had escaped them. Now they joined those who had handkerchiefs over their nostrils and mouths to smother the smell of decaying flesh and from time to time fanned flies that were thickly present.

A woman they instantly recognized as Miss Martha detached herself from the procession and knelt on the ground beside the body of her son.

"Murder! Murder! Murder!" she chanted.

As if on cue, others responded, "We want justice! We want justice!"

This call-and-response incantation continued for some five minutes, with other mourners adding intermittent comments.

"Who is going to bury wi dead?"

"Where dem tek we pickney dem?"

"How we going to get di body dem to the dead house?"

As the procession's rhetorical questions came thick and fast, the security officers stood guard close by, guns at the ready. The women were defiant, challenging the Executive Arm of the State to provide answers to the impasse in view of the failure of any other official to put in an appearance in the community.

Suddenly, a young woman seemed to snap. She pulled off her blonde wig, tore off her dress and underwear, and started screaming as if she was "in the spirit," as Pentecostal churchgoers put it. Running up to a soldier, she pummeled his chest with her fists, disregarding his drawn gun and the shouts of caution from the grief-stricken but fearful crowd.

In startling reflex action, the soldier pushed her to the ground and, still holding his gun, unzipped his fly, pulled out an erect penis, and in front of the mourners and fellow security officers who seemed equally stunned and too shocked to respond, forced himself into the wildly flaying woman and started to hump her in vicious thrusts. It did not take him long to come to orgasm. Heaving himself off the now uncontrollably hysterical woman, he replaced his diminished member, zipped up his fly, raised his gun, and said coldly into the crowd, "Anybody else want some a mi?"

It was as if he had poured acid into fresh wounds. In seconds, the soldier was being pelted with any object the mourners could lay their hands on, from stones to shoes, sticks, and bottles of water. The wails, curses, and body explosions combined was like the turning eye of a hurricane. With equal fury, the crowd advanced on the soldier, who held his gun as a shield. Undeterred, a young man ran toward him with a ratchet knife drawn, intent on doing grievous bodily harm to the violator. He almost hit his mark but was stopped in his tracks by a bullet to the forehead, and as he was falling, the offending soldier let off an automatic round, riddling the body of the youth, who was dead before he hit the ground.

This had provided sufficient distraction for the advancing crowd. Overpowered by numbers, the soldier was soon on the ground next to the youth he had murdered, his gun pried loose of his struggling fingers as in unison, about thirty persons succeeded in clobbering him to a bloody pulp.

All this happened so swiftly that the soldier's colleagues were unsure how to react. Finally, a khaki-clad officer raised his rifle and fired a round of shots into the air, which had the desired effect. The bloodletting eased, and the hysteria subsided. Someone brought a sheet and covered the rape victim and led her away, still shrieking. Over a loudspeaker, a soldier announced, "This is Sergeant House. You are to disperse and return to your houses immediately. Right now! Everyone off the streets! There is to be no gathering on the streets! If anyone is seen out here in ten minutes, I swear to God, in the name of law and order, you will be shot."

The distraught citizens heard the seriousness in his voice, and for emphasis, the man fired another round. This was enough to encourage everyone to make haste and heed his command, leaving the objects of their mourning lying in the street. By the time Kwame was bounding up the stairs, his mother was already descending the stairway, her anxiety at the commotion causing her to tremble.

"Inside, inside!" She dragged her son into the apartment and slammed the door shut.

Although the streets cleared quickly, the seething anger was evident in the furious calls that residents placed to friends, family members, and public institutions such as the media, churches, Jamaicans for Justice, the new Jamaica Council for Human Rights, Women's Media

Watch, and the Kingston Public Hospital. Residents were so used to violations of their human rights, they were constantly bombarding these institutions with complaints.

Sometimes these protests yielded positive results, although more often than not, while they secured sympathy, this concern did not always translate into action. Even in cases where something was done to ease a crisis, the action was seldom transformative. This led to a culture of cynicism at the ground level, but under the circumstances, those with phone contacts to the various agencies still felt impelled to do something and let those outside their virtual prison (constructed as they are, in typical projects style, with footprints of two- and three-story walk-ups), know what was going on.

Meanwhile, back in the street, the soldiers had retrieved the body of their colleague and secured it in an army truck. It was going to take great courage to explain his death to the Joint Chief of Staff. Sergeant House, the man in charge of the security operation, delegated to a detail of ten soldiers and four policemen the responsibility of taking the sheet-wrapped bodies to the May Pen Cemetery to bury them. He then called the chief to update him on the recent turn of events.

The sergeant felt hesitation in his heart as he began, but his voice was firm.

"Chief, we have an emergency situation. The people were demonstrating in the street with some of the bodies of their relatives when a woman just went stark raving mad and attacked Corporal Brown, and after that, another man attacked him, and he had to defend himself. And after that, the people attacked him, Sir, and he is gone."

"Are you sure you are not leaving out anything from your report, Sergeant?" The voice of the chief was grim on the other end, and it sent a chill down Sergeant House's spine. He hesitated a moment before continuing and opted to add the grave detail he had omitted, with some polish.

"Well, Sir, it seems as if the pressure of the operation got to Corporal Brown, and he took out his frustration on the mad woman who attacked him. I mean, Sir," the sergeant stammered almost pleadingly, "we have all been under a lot of pressure—"

The chief cut in. "Sergeant, you had better sort out your onions fast because it seems as if the residents have called he, she, and the old lady and told them about the corporal raping the woman at gunpoint in public view. Concealing that information from me makes you an accessory after the fact and liable for court martial."

The sergeant was silent, thinking fast. How could he tell the chief that he had ordered bodies to be buried without consultation with higher authorities? *I am in a real stew now*, he thought but again was firm when he spoke.

"I would like an urgent face-to-face discussion with you, Chief. There are other things that I cannot mention on the phone."

"Well, you had better arrange for Inspector Greaves to hold the fort and you get here as quickly as possible. I am recommending that the curfew be extended with immediate effect. As a matter of fact, negotiations are now underway for the imposition of a state of emergency because the situation is deemed to be out of control. The fugitive is not in custody, and that is not acceptable. We can discuss the casualty figures when you get here." With that instruction, the chief ended the call.

"It is going to be a long night," Sergeant House muttered to himself.

The news of the renewed curfew and the impending state of emergency hit the Tivoli Gardens residents with a bang. Women, men, boys, and girls were glued to the seven o'clock news on television; mercifully, the light and power company had not disconnected the services this time around. The news anchor paused from speculating on the whereabouts of Dudus and announced, *"We interrupt this news item to bring you a breaking news story, and we must warn viewers that the footage we are about to show is not recommended for children under the age of sixteen years—even for teenagers in this category, parental guidance is advised because the images are very disturbing.*

"The amateur filming was done on a Blackberry phone by a resident of the Tivoli Gardens community and sent to our newsroom by internet connection a few moments ago. We repeat—this footage is highly sensitive, but under the circumstances, our editorial team deemed its broadcast is in the national interest."

The footage from the mourning scene and all that followed played on the screen. If a census had been taken over the entire island during the episode until the forced dispersal of the crowd, it is probable that no one would have heard a pin drop. When the newscaster resumed, it was to note that speculation was rife about the fate of the bodies that the residents had to abandon in the streets.

"In addition," he added, *"Legal questions are being raised about the autonomy with which the security forces are operating as well as the impunity shown by the soldier in his response to the grief of the residents, who are alleging that there have been other experiences of excess during the three-day operation. So far, no body count has been made available to the media, although residents claim they have confirmed the deaths of several residents and nonresidents, as well as the forced removal of several men from the community. This station will bring you updates as this situation unfolds."*

At the live broadcast of the Saturday afternoon events in Tivoli Gardens, pandemonium broke out at

Up Park Camp army headquarters and at the office of the Commissioner of Police. Telephones were ringing in every office; cell phones were also ringing as government officials placed direct calls to the officers in charge of the on-the-ground operations. The blame game was being played on all sides.

Assuming the role of his moniker, the Public Defender placed several calls to the Prime Minister's cell phone, which, understandably, was constantly busy. He managed to get through to the Leader of the Opposition, the Governor General, the head of the Jamaica Council of Churches, the head of the Private Sector Organisation and the head of the Peace Management Initiative and suggested that they attend an emergency meeting the next day at the Pegasus Hotel to discuss the grave turn of events and consider steps to be taken in the public interest. They all agreed that the situation was of sufficient emergency to warrant such an urgent gathering, and the meeting was set for two o'clock in the afternoon. There was national consensus that delaying of damage control was politically unconscionable.

By the time Sergeant House arrived at Up Park Camp, the chief was livid and seemed to be chewing fire when the man entered his office.

"You see what I was talking about now, you see, you see?" he shouted. "How you really think that make us look, eh?

How you think that make us look?" He had the habit of repeating himself when he was very angry.

From experience, Sergeant House kept silent until the edge had worn off his boss's anger. Then he said, "Chief, we will have to do some damage control. We need to send a press release to the media and explain the constraints under which we have been operating and the fact that we had to defend ourselves in the face of attack on us by gunmen and civilians alike..." His voice trailed off as the chief exploded.

"You just don't get it, do you? First of all, we lack the public's confidence. They just do not believe our side of the story anymore, and to try to tell them to take our side now after what they just saw on TV would be suicidal."

The chief paused and, reaching for the telephone on his desk, dialed Major Butler's number and requested that he and Inspector Wright come to his office immediately. Both Butler and Wright were known to be the army thugs who facilitated the disappearance of troublesome officers. The dampness that was creeping under Sergeant House's armpits now broke out into open sweat, but the chief was not finished.

"I also just got a call from the mayor. He tells me that you were burning bodies in the community and burying others in May Pen Cemetery. Is there any truth to this?"

The question hung like an inverted glacier between the men for about five seconds, and Sergeant House was about to respond when the summoned officers walked through the open office door.

"Well, is it true?" the chief bellowed.

"Yes, Sir," the beleaguered sergeant responded.

At this admission, it seemed that the chief was going to do an Incredible Hulk act and burst out of his seams. With effort, he contained himself and continued the interrogation.

"Once the curfew was lifted, did you make arrangements for the undertakers to come in and collect the bodies?"

"I did not receive any orders to do that, Sir."

"But you are in charge, man!" the chief roared.

The sergeant was too numb to reply.

"Take him away," the chief instructed the newcomers. "He is to be held under high security conditions, twenty-four seven."

Sergeant House was so dazed by this turn of events that he shouted in turn, "So, Chief, you are going to make me a scapegoat? I was covering for the whole of us—the whole country, as a matter of fact."

The chief responded frigidly, "If you don't watch your mouth, House, I will also charge you with insubordination."

As he was led away by his peers, Sergeant House thought bitterly that the chief was performing like a real backra massa with his divide-and-rule tactics.

Chapter Nine

WHILE THE SAGA surrounding Christopher Dudus Coke was of national interest, for those far removed from the scene of the crime so to speak, it was almost background noise, which they hoped would soon be turned off. However, the live broadcast of the rape scene and its wide-reaching implications made the entire drama of immediate individual concern. The political ripple effect competed with the shock waves spreading among ordinary Jamaicans as well as those directly involved. Sentiments related to the oft-repeated cry of "we want justice" dominated conversations in every walk of life from Saturday night through to Sunday morning.

On Sunday, several pastors abandoned their prepared sermons and instead conferred with their distraught congregations and offered mass counseling sessions to assuage the widespread sense of violation being expressed in all quarters. While government officials tried with public statements and press releases to repair the damage, civil society coalesced around the call for the Prime Minister's resignation.

This call was one of the main items on the agenda of the hastily convened meeting organized the previous evening by the Public Defender. The Commissioner of Police and the Chief of Staff of the Jamaica Defense Force both reported that they were close to making a breakthrough in their efforts to capture Dudus. However, for security reasons, the details of this operation were still classified. The Minister of Information, speaking on behalf of the Prime Minister, who sent his apologies for not attending due to his surprise tour of the Tivoli Gardens community to directly address the residents' concerns, endorsed this position. He emphasized that the national interest was of highest priority and that the joint police/military operation had the full backing of the government. When the Public Defender raised the issue of the televised Tivoli Gardens violations, the Minister of Information reported that a statement would be issued from the Office of the Prime Minister after the conclusion of the Prime Minister's visit to the troubled community.

The Jamaicans for Justice representative cited the legal ramifications of the happenings broadcast on the previous night's newscast, which the Women's Media Watch spokesperson endorsed, emphasizing that always, under war conditions, women's bodies become vessels of defilement, reinforcing the connections between violence against women as a sociocultural concern and the implicit endorsement of such abuse by the state when their representatives carried out such acts. The debate that ensued became so heated that the Public Defender had to intervene to cool rising tempers.

When the Public Defender flagged the issue of the chorus of calls that had been issued by various public institutions for the Prime Minister to step down, the Minister of Information indicated that it was an issue the Prime Minister would also mention when he made his address to the nation that evening.

The Chief of Staff then said, "Whatever happens, now that we are in Tivoli, which is a situation that had been impossible when Dudus was there, we have no intention of leaving. I have therefore recommended to the Prime Minister that we convert the curfew to a state of emergency for the maximum period allowed under the law, and he agreed. That should be part of his address to the nation."

The Minister of Information concurred; however, the Jamaicans for Justice representative objected, noting that as the television broadcast had indicated, the occupation of the community by the security forces had led to serious human rights violations, which needed urgent redress.

The Public Defender agreed, adding, "Implementing a state of emergency should not be a unilateral decision but should be done in consultation with civic bodies who can monitor the process to safeguard the interests of the citizens concerned. We will also need to set up a Commission of Enquiry so that the truth about the events of the past three days can be ventilated."

"With all due respect," the Commissioner of Police interjected, "this situation calls for drastic measures, and there is no time for consultation and that kind of dilly-dallying. The country is in crisis over this affair, and we must respond with speed. Speaking of which, if you will excuse me, I have to leave as—" indicating the Blackberry device in his hand "—I see some urgent messages on my phone." With that, he left.

The Public Defender cleared his throat and said, "Well, I think we have raised the main issues this meeting was called to address. The next step is to investigate the publicized incident and to follow the procedure to ensure that the Commission of Enquiry into allegations of misconduct of the security forces is organized and the violations of human rights addressed. Anyone having any other opinion on these matters should direct them to my office, which is going to be open on a twenty-four-hour basis for at least the next week."

After discussions that lasted for a further twenty minutes, the meeting broke up and the participants left.

Back in Tivoli Gardens, the residents were trying to pick up the pieces of their shattered nerves. Bishop Walters and his brethren mobilized the residents by phone to have a prayer vigil from noon to three o'clock in the afternoon. The residents could be heard praying and occasionally bursting out in song and praise. The word that the bishop sent out was based on the biblical injunction that *"We wrestle not against flesh and blood, but against principalities, against powers, against rulers of the darkness of this world, against spiritual wickedness in high places."* By cell phone, the message was conveyed that despite being confined to their homes, the residents should feel free to lift their voices in supplication to the Almighty for deliverance.

The security officers were astounded that in contrast to the cowering behind closed doors which had characterized the residents' demeanor in the initial stages of the Incursion, there was a sustained volume of lamentations throughout the community in the designated period. Since this was happening indoors, there was nothing they could do. Bishop Walters had facilitated the emergence of a form of civil disobedience that provided the residents with a vital outlet for their frustrations.

It may have been sheer coincidence or Divine intervention that the Prime Minister's party arrived to tour the community at three-thirty, but the residents gave him the benefit of the doubt. Word of the presence of the officials spread on the informal network. Eugenie's brother called and informed her to keep the information quiet, but because she was in Miss Martha's apartment when the call came and the phone was on speaker, the publication of the news was inevitable. Miss Martha was doubly grieving about the loss of her son and the disappearance of the bodies from the street, and she was keeping secrets for no one.

The worshippers saw the arrival of officials to survey the community as a direct answer to their prayers, but before they had time to rejoice, residents who spied the party from upper-floor vantage points reported that the company was leaving as swiftly as it had come. After brief discussions with the officers in charge, there being no residents in sight, the Prime Minister left with his entourage at four o'clock. His instructions were that the tight security cordon was to be maintained around the community.

The internal buzz among Tivoli Gardens residents was heightened when, at six-thirty, instead of the usual personality program on the television, the prerecorded show was replaced by a reporter.

"We apologize for interrupting our regularly scheduled program to announce that following intense investigations, the security forces have succeeded in capturing the fugitive Don of Tivoli Gardens, Christopher Dudus Coke, in a covert operation along the main highway leading into Kingston. Disguised as a woman, he was being driven by a prominent clergyman who alleges that Coke was on his way to the United States embassy to surrender.

"The police also report that based on intelligence, Coke's whereabouts were pinpointed earlier this week, and today, he was tailed for hours before the police finally closed

in and captured him. The strongman put up very little resistance. Adjusting his wig and other attire as he was ordered to step out of the back of the vehicle in which he was traveling, he presented a comical image for someone who is alleged to have legendary influence in the drug and gun running worlds.

"Witnesses say that Coke had tears in his eyes as he was handcuffed and led away to a security vehicle while pulling up his stockings. His lawyer has indicated that he will waive his rights to stand trial in local courts and instead will be extradited to the United States to face the charges that have been brought against him.

"Meanwhile the security forces have indicated that, with the capture of Coke, they will lift the curfew imposed on the Tivoli Gardens Community tomorrow. However, the Prime Minister is scheduled to address the nation tonight on the matter, and in a press release, Jamaica House has noted that he is positively considering accepting the recommendation from the security forces to implement a state of emergency with immediate effect. We will notify the public as soon as further details on this developing story are available."

A wave of mixed reactions met this latest disclosure. On the one hand, among those sympathetic to Coke, there was disappointment that he had met such an ignominious fate. The effeminized imagery of the wigged and bespectacled fugitive diminished previous descriptions of him as a strongman and leader of the infamous international Shower Posse. On the other hand, those who saw him in a more unfavorable light found the switch nothing short of hilarious.

In Tivoli Gardens, relief that the capture of the Don, which signaled an end to the traumatic ordeal of the confrontation between security forces and gunmen was, inevitably, also mixed with contempt at the diminishing of the figure in whose thrall they had existed for years. Relief at this dramatic turn of events was also tinged with unbridled humor at the ridiculous representation embodied by the disguise in which he had been caught.

Like other children in the community, Kwame was relieved when Monday morning dawned and the normalcy of a school day presented itself. He left home at seven o'clock, half an hour earlier than usual, in order to stop by Brother Ken's to discuss the turn of events. His mentor gave him a warm hug, and they both mingled thoughts on the long road of recovery ahead of the community as it addressed the healing of the wounds inflicted on mind, body, and soul by the past week's events.

Kwame was about to leave when he remembered the secondary reason for his detour.

"Oh, I forgot to tell you, Brother Ken," he said with some excitement. "I am going to enter the debating competition coming up at school, and I am going to be opposing the moot that dancehall is the obstacle to youth having positive values and attitudes in Jamaica today."

"Oh?" Brother Ken looked up from the pile of CDs that he had been sifting through. "And what will be the main thrust of your argument?"

"I am going to show that dancehall is the creative melting pot of the inner city, that it contains all the desires that the outer city is too hypocritical to admit and provides a space for those who are invisible because they live in the ghetto. I think that the women who make themselves naked and skin out under the video lights are using their bodies to tell a story about how difficult life is because of poverty, and instead of behaving like people uptown, they are showing that because life is so hard here, we have to create new rules for ourselves.

"I am also going to explain that dancehall allows poor youth to make money from careers that would be impossible, as employers refuse ghetto youth jobs because of their address. So, by becoming deejays, dancers, singers and making their own fashion they are being very creative—"

Brother Ken interrupted his protégée's impassioned defense by asking, "How will you respond to the critics who say that dancehall is just dry sex that passes for dancing?"

Sensing an element of devil's advocacy in the question, Kwame thought hard for a moment. Finally, he said, "People go to the dancehall to enjoy themselves. The dry sex dances serve as a safe sex option for people who are very honest about how they relate to their bodies. Sex is not as taboo to people in inner-city communities as it is in many uptown areas. Sex is talked about freely, and people feel no way to have it in any style or pattern. I have heard women cursing about who is taking whose man, for example, and about how good they are at doing sex and what they can do to hold a man. When women are modeling in their crews, they talk a lot about sex.

"Sex also is part of the way they dress and handle their bodies on the dance floor. Having the baddest wine is what they use to show their power. But I am not saying that all inner-city people are the same thing or act in the same way. What I am saying is that there are differences among people in the inner city just like in the outer city."

Again, Brother Ken interrupted with a critical question. "Isn't it men who control women's sexuality when it is the men who are the judges of whether women have the best wine or wickedest slam? What say you to that, my son?"

Kwame considered his mentor's question, then responded, "I often wonder why women would dress in the skimpiest of clothes often with no panties on and do all those skin out dances even standing on their head tops under the video lights for all the world to see. It does make it seem that the women are slack and trying to attract men so they can get money from them by having sex. Yes, that is one side of the story, but you can also look at it another way. People who are black and poor have no say in societies like ours, so it is difficult to recognize that what they are doing is fighting against the system. But I really think that is what they are doing. They are trying to be seen. They want to get any attention, by any means necessary, rather than no attention at all.

"I know it sounds kind of sick, but they *are* sick when you really think about it. It is the deep psychological sickness that they are suffering from that makes many women and more and more men in the ghetto bleach their skins because they believe this improves their appearance and status."

They were both silent for a while, contemplating the implications of the issues they were addressing. Finally, Brother Ken asked a combination of questions to encourage the young debater to push his argument further.

"What about love? Where does love fit into all of this? And is it possible for those who take part in these explicit dancehall activities to be religiously inclined?"

"Oh, that's a tough one," Kwame admitted. "I guess some people think sex and love are the same thing, but because others are so poor, they use their bodies to gain scarce resources. Poverty and area stigma make them desperate.

But this does not mean that they do not love. They love… their families, their friends…themselves! And they also love God because many were brought up in the Church and even go to church too. It is all very complicated."

Just then, Kwame saw the twinkle in Brother Ken's eyes and realized that all the questions were designed to get him to examine whether he was going to make a useful contribution to the proposed debate. They both burst into laughter because Brother Ken's ruse had been so effective.

"You pass this round," Brother Ken managed to say. "I guess you are ready for the debate. I won't miss being in that audience for the world."

Chapter Ten

IT WAS THREE years since the Incursion, but to people in Tivoli Gardens who still suffered the trauma of reliving their acrid memories, it seemed as if it were only yesterday. It was doubly frustrating for those who had poured out their stories to the Public Defender hoping to get redress but were still waiting for justice for their loss of loved ones, property, peace of mind, and an era of political largesse. The community had changed from being a fortress against the security forces to occupied territory; the police post that was supposed to have been a temporary installation to restore order in the aftermath of the hostilities, had become a permanent fixture of the government's policy of "curb and control." It was therefore surprising that lawlessness had once again snaked its insidious way onto the social landscape and had silently subverted the uneasy peace that had prevailed since that fateful May in 2010.

Everyone in the Tivoli Gardens community agreed, as if by osmosis, that it was living with the painful memories that was the hardest part of trying to move on with their lives after the Tivoli Incursion. As Kemesha— Sadie Baynes' granddaughter by her deceased daughter

Sophia, one of the casualties of the Tivoli Incursion—sat in classes at the Mico University College where she was now a second-year student, having passed six CXCs with Grade 1 and one with Grade 2, it was hard for any of her classmates who did not come from an inner-city community to even begin to comprehend what she and her family had gone through during those fateful days in the immediate aftermath of the incident and even now, three years later. None of them suspected the radical changes that people in Kemesha's community had had to cope with. There were days when she had to escape to the bathroom to relieve herself of pent-up emotions with a good cry, and if she felt strong enough, she would return to classes, thanking her lucky stars that she wore glasses so people could not really see her discomfiture. Having to explain exposed her to the prying questions that usually followed whenever she revealed her geographical origins. As she had told her sister Tameka when they spoke the day before, "You can get away from a location or a person, but when thoughts invade your mind, there is no escape."

Kemesha knew only too well just how unsettling those memory invasions, as she called them, could be. She felt as if she were rushing down a waterfall which had no end and from which she could not escape except by plunging herself into extremely consuming activities. She still had to exercise tremendous discipline to halt the memory rush through multiple corridors of could-have-beens, if-I-did-knows and if-only-I-could-haves. These memory invasions happened involuntarily on particularly poignant occasions, like her mother's birthday on March 22; this year was especially worrying because her unusually heavy menstrual cycle started on that same date.

"I had a very normal period only two weeks before," she confided to Tameka, "so I really wasn't expecting it so soon, and it came in thick clots for the whole day and stopped just after midnight. It was weird. I almost feel as if Mummy was invading me to make me remember her, but I wasn't planning to forget. I never knew anything could hurt so much and for so long. With that one-day period, Tameka, the next day you couldn't believe that I did not have a sign of what had happened the day before, so is not like I could even go to the doctor to explain the symptoms because they are gone. But I can't help it. Certain things just trigger my depression."

"It's the same for me," her sister had replied. They had both become strict vegetarians, since neither could tolerate the sight or smell of cooking flesh, which they associated with their mother, whose decomposing body had remained in their apartment for two days before Corporal Clarke could arrange for the government pathologist to come and perform an on-the-spot postmortem and remove the body to the morgue.

"I can't sleep properly either," Tameka said, and Kemesha now remembered their sister Kaylia had said that too. "I dream about it every night and sometimes it is just a smell that sends me off." Tameka described how she had vomited and fainted at her school's barbecue the previous evening and left prematurely because although she thought that she could tolerate the smell of roasting meat, at a distance, in the open air, she still hyperventilated. She associated that odor with the acrid stench of burning human flesh that residents believed had pervaded the atmosphere the night the security forces had stormed the barricades—that fateful night when their mother died.

Several persons in Tivoli Gardens who still could not locate the remains of their loved ones concluded that the thick rumors of bodies being burned, alongside evidence of hasty burials, were true. Like other community residents, Kemesha and Tameka acknowledged that no matter how hard they tried to block out the memories, recollections of those horrors were beyond their control. Even outside stimulants had the power to trigger these memories, which rushed into their thoughts and emotions, threatening to drown them.

Inevitably, the sisters also spoke of their sibling Kaylia's successful suicide after the second attempt. She had been particularly close to her mother; they were telepathic in a remarkable way.

"I always feel that I should have seen it coming," Kemesha said in reference to their sister's jump from the roof of Building C, where her boyfriend lived, on the second anniversary of the Incursion. "Even though it was a year ago, I am still dreaming about that too."

"Especially since she had taken the pills on the same date the year before that," Tameka agreed. "She was really crying for help."

Marlon Pryce, the ex-boyfriend of their now-deceased sister, had told them that Kaylia had made the most passionate love with him around eight o'clock that night and then, when he fell asleep, she wrote him a note, at nine-fifteen, to inform him of her intention to jump because, she said, she "could not live with the memory of witnessing what had happened to her mother." She elaborated that although she was engaged to be married to him, she was also terrified of the prospect of having babies and having to go through what her mother experienced. "In a way, what she do was cold," Marlon had said at the funeral, "but I understand because apart from the injustices that we suffered during the Incursion, there is no help for people like Kaylia who have experienced different forms of trauma. The authorities may have paid out some money for damage to property, but I don't think anyone can compensate us for the loss of our peace of mind."

Steve had also made a speech at the funeral, weeping openly and admitting that he had "made a mistake" by not standing beside Sophia and his stepdaughters before, during, and after the Incursion—"like a real man should have." He was particularly remorseful for not being there for her the night of the Incursion and used the occasion of Kaylia's funeral to confess and beg for forgiveness.

"I just have to say that Sadie saved the day," he concluded. "Somehow, she found a way to keep our baby alive, and I am committing my life to taking care of her the way that a real man should. Big man ting."

The church had burst into supportive applause because it was by then common knowledge that despite the unwholesome circumstances, Sadie fought the odds to save the baby's life.

When she took the pulpit, Sadie was unapologetic that she "had a sermon to preach," because she had not managed to have closure for her daughter since her body had disappeared without trace from the morgue and they had been thwarted in their attempts to regain it, preventing the family from having the closure that a burial would have afforded.

"But God who see and know all things will give the unjust their just reward," she declared, "and every unfair game..."

"Must play over," the congregation concluded in unison.

"Oh, yes!" Sadie reiterated. "For the Lord knoweth the ways of the righteous, but the ways of the ungodly shall perish. What happened was not just about the President. It was an assault on us as poor people by the state because they consider that when we are weak, we need to depend on them. Kaylia was not able to be strong. She yielded to the temptation to be weak, and though she was my grandchild, I cannot say I condone what she did, but believe me, I understand why her spirit could break under the weight of the burden we have to bear."

"Amen to that, my sister!" A dreadlocked woman who everyone recognized as Madda Terese, whose hair touched the ground on the few occasions she let it out, shouted from the congregation and spontaneously interrupted Sadie's sermon by singing,

> No night in Zion there is no night there no night in Zion there is no night there, no night in Zion, there is no night there

> For Selassie I is INI light, INI don't need no candlelight, Halelu-Jah there is no night there

The congregation joined in for two more rounds of this singing rendition before again focusing on Sadie's elaborate remembrance speech.

"My granddaughter Kaylia is gone, but we are here, and we must go on. My granddaughter Destiny survived by a miracle, so we all can too. For three days, we were unable to feed her anything but coconut water, and by God! She survived in the belly of the beast because as you know, bredrin and sistren, dem did lef we fi dead down here. But what no dead no call it duppy. It was like Bob Marley say…"

She called, "He who fights and runs away," and the congregation responded, "Lives to fight another day!"

By talking to each other several times a day, every day, on their postpaid and text credit accounts, Kemesha and Tameka were part of a broader social support network that helped ease the constant pain.

Tameka had moved in with her grandmother and youngest sister in Old Harbour, where she preferred the slower pace of life compared to the heat and rapid-response requirements of the city. She excelled at both academic and cocurricular activities and so had earned the coveted position of Top Prefect in just under two years.

"Corporal Clarke called me today," said Kemesha into her phone to Tameka. "He sold the first batch of sweet peppers from his greenhouse." After he was court-martialed for insubordination, desertion, and collaborating with community residents during the Tivoli Gardens Incursion, Clarke returned to his native Manchester, where he was a farmer. However, he was shocked to realize that during the years he was stationed in Kingston, the face of his community in Broadleaf had changed drastically due to fallout from the bauxite industry. Most farmers had lost their livelihoods and were dependent on remittances to purchase food due to loss of land and soil depletion.

Clarke therefore introduced state-of-the-art technology to provide employment and a model for alternative community development, which was proving successful. He had adopted Sadie and her grandchildren as his own family and was grateful they had accepted him as such. They had stood by him when the institution he had served for eight years had so severely punished him for standing up for the human rights of the citizens and expressing public remorse for the wrongs he had done. At the disciplinary hearing, the corporal had confessed to the crimes he had committed, but rather than accept responsibility, his superiors had struck his confession off the record and indicted him for a shorter period than was necessary. Clarke recognized the leniency as mere cover-up for the culpability of his superiors whose orders he had been following.

***

The day after Kaylia's funeral, Sadie went to the Public Defender's office and demanded to see him.

"Do you have an appointment?" his secretary asked. "Is he expecting you?"

Sadie felt some choice words rising in her throat, and they were about to roll off her tongue when she bit them back and instead said, in the most dulcet tones she could muster, "He is expecting me."

"What is your name?" the secretary, Ms. Loris Davis inquired.

"Sadie Baynes."

The secretary entered the inner sanctum of the Public Defender's office and shut the door. Hurriedly, Sadie closed the distance between where she had been standing in the foyer and the door behind which the secretary had disappeared so that she could listen to what was being said on the other side.

"A woman by the name of Sadie Baynes said that you are expecting her, Sir."

"Baynes? But she is not in my appointment book—" the Public Defender started, and both he and Ms. Davis were shocked when Sadie opened the unlocked door and walked in. The Public Defender recognized her immediately; Sadie had reported what had happened with Sophia, Destiny, and Henry, of whom no one could find any trace. Henry's shop had also been vandalized; several bullet holes in the door and walls told their own gruesome tale.

"Mr. Public Defender, I do not have to be in your appointment book. I want to be on your conscience, not in your appointment book. I want you to know that I buried my granddaughter yesterday. She committed suicide as a result of being unable to bear the memories of what happened during the Incursion. She was not able to wrap her mind around a future, although she was young and had her whole life ahead of her. She was stuck in that episode, and we were not able to afford the sort of psychological support needed to bring her into the present and convince her it was over. But the truth is, it is not over for us. It is something we will always live with. So you know that it is serious, not just what happened in 2010 but the effect it has been having even as we try to move forward. My brother, we need for you to act and be our defender. We want justice, we want compensation. We want retribution, recompense, and restitution. More than anything else, though, we need the public to know what we have to deal with and what we are facing."

The Public Defender heaved a huge sigh and spread his hands almost helplessly.

"Ms. Baynes, I feel your pain, like I feel the pain of all the victims of this atrocity. But as you can see, I need help myself. It was a major problem to produce my interim report and to make the public aware of what you and so many other people have experienced. What you are addressing shows that the state is guilty, and it has precedence. But you have to give me some time so that we can get the resources to get the reports out and raise awareness about your plight."

"You don't realize what I am saying, sir? It is too late! It is too late for you, for me—for all of us. Today is the last day that I can wait for my justice. This is my time now!"

With that declaration, Sadie opened her handbag, pulled out a handgun, and before the secretary or Public Defender realized her intention, she raised the weapon and shot the Public Defender in his forehead, straight between his eyes. Ms. Davis let out a bloodcurdling scream as her boss collapsed to the floor. Sadie turned to the secretary and, before her scream ended, cut off her voice with a single bullet to her mouth, silencing her forever.

When she had left home on her mission of death that morning, Sadie never doubted for a minute that she had to do something drastic to ease the all-too-familiar pain that now lived permanently in the region of her womb—a pain she knew was reflected, many times over, in many others, waiting for some action toward their compensation. However, as Bertha said when the community support group met the previous week, "A donation from the government to individuals to fix mashed-up furniture or re-plaster walls dug out by policemen's and soldiers' bullets is not compensation."

As she replaced the gun in her handbag, changed her blouse, skirt, shoes, and wig, Sadie thought to herself that maybe the media would now pay more attention to their plight; they only responded when someone they considered important was killed.

"But to them, we don't count," she muttered out loud. "Not until now."

With that, she carefully wiped off the door handles to remove her fingerprints and let herself out into the street.

About the Author

Dr. Imani Tafari-Ama is currently Research Fellow at the Regional Coordinating Office for the Institute for Gender and Development Studies, having just completed a year as Fulbright Scholar-in-Residence at Bridgewater State University in Massachusetts. Previous to that assignment, Imani was International Fellow and Curator at the Flensburg Maritime Museum (2016–17), tasked with formulating an African-Caribbean analysis of Danish Colonialism and Legacy in Flensburg, the Virgin Islands of the United States and Ghana, culminating in the Rum, Sweat and Tears exhibition (June 2017–March 2018).

With a PhD in Development Studies and Master's degree in Women and Development Studies, Dr. Imani Tafari-Ama has lectured across a broad range of disciplines and on a number of topics including: feminist methodology/epistemology, action research and the policy process, the culture of Rastafari and African religious retentions in the Caribbean, thought and action in the African Diaspora, Dancehall, sex and religious ideology and culture and community development, as well as being invited to give special lectures on colonial history, violence and gender and development issues and Rastafari at institutions around the world.

Dr. Imani Tafari-Ama is the author of: *Blood, Bullets and Bodies: Sexual Politics Below Jamaica's Poverty Line, Up for Air: This Half Has Never Been Told* (an award-winning novel; https://youtu.be/qQNYGjRFlwk) and *Lead in the Veins* (poetry) as well as several book chapters and articles. She is also a multimedia journalist who has produced several audio-visual documentaries including "Setting the Skin Tone," which explores the catastrophic social practice of skin bleaching (https://youtu.be/VNwIZ_xHjm0). This eight-and-a-half-minute video documentary (produced in 2006) is an excerpt from her doctoral research.

Website: https://imanitafariama.com

Beaten Track Publishing

For more titles from Beaten Track Publishing, please visit our website:

https://www.beatentrackpublishing.com

Thanks for reading!